DEATH HAS COME UP INTO OUR WINDOWS

Published by 47North
P.O. Box 400818
Las Vegas, NV 89140

ISBN-13: 9781612185828
ISBN-10: 1612185827

DEATH HAS COME UP INTO OUR WINDOWS

BASED LOOSELY ON THE EVENTS OF JEREMIAH · 595 BC

THE ZOMBIE BIBLE

BY

STANT LITORE

47N★RTH

For all our forebears who labored
in pursuit of a better world

CONTENTS

Historian's Note • IX

First Day: Truth at the Bottom of the Well • 1

Second Day: If All God's People Were Prophets • 46

Third Day: Wind in the Dark • 72

Third Night: As Papyrus Burns • 77

HISTORIAN'S NOTE

THE CRISIS created by an outbreak of the walking dead offers a telling diagnostic of those flaws in the human condition that resurface, century upon century: our tendency to let problems fester untended until they become crises, our frequent inability to work together for a common good, our quickness to forget the lessons our grandparents learned at the cost of much sweat and blood, and the extent to which our privileged classes ignore and deny responsibility for the plight of the impoverished and the disinherited. Our ancestors often described the attacks of the hungry dead as acts of either divine retribution for human sins or divine abandonment in utter grief at human evil, and in at least one sense they may have been correct: the rapid rise of an outbreak is nearly always a consequence of our own failings.

    Even across a gap of millennia, those scrolls attributed to the prophet Yirmiyahu (whose name we anglicize as "Jeremiah") retain their power both to evoke the memory of one of history's most tragic outbreaks of the zombie plague and to move our hearts with one of history's most eloquent appeals for social justice. A minimum of historical context may suffice to set the stage for our narrative. As a levite's son, Yirmiyahu was a member of the privileged class of the priesthood, though he was born in a small village; moving early in his life to the more urban center of Yerusalem, Yirmiyahu was apparently appalled at the level of poverty he witnessed there. Taking up the role of a prophet—a navi, *or bringer of words from God—he began to preach in the streets and on the Temple steps, demanding that the city dwellers return to the terms of their ancestors' Covenant with their deity—specifically, communal provision for orphans and widows, monotheism, abstention from human sacrifice, clean burial for the dead, and the observing of a periodic year of* yovel *in which all slaves and indentured workers would be released from their bondage or their debts.*

At about the same time, the youthful king of the Hebrews, Zedekiah, ceased paying tribute to Babylon in the east—and then used the savings in large part to garrison the city against a possible invasion. That invasion came swiftly, and Babylon established a lengthy and debilitating siege. Food stores within the city ran low, and in the overcrowded conditions created by the hurried evacuation of the surrounding countryside prior to the siege, an outbreak of the dead (who had never fully been cleaned out of the city's back alleys) surged unchecked. Yirmiyahu believed that this situation, taken together with the injustice and corruption of Yerusalem's leaders, made holding the city untenable—and that the only course of action that would merit God's favor and forgiveness would be to surrender the gates of the city and beseech the aid of the Babylonians in cleansing the city of the dead and feeding its famished populace. Yirmiyahu's very public voicing of this opinion did not make him popular with the king and the merchant class, who in a surrender would lose everything.

In this crisis there was a terrible irony, one likely not lost on the prophet. A century earlier, Yerusalem had faced a similar siege and its population had been similarly outnumbered and locked within the city's narrow walls; yet the earlier siege had crumbled when the pestilence raged through the enemy camp, so that the enemy turned and devoured one another. The walls of Yerusalem had sufficed to keep out the enemy, both living and dead. In the generations since, these events had become a bedside story of divine deliverance that mothers related to their children.

Doubtless, the king and the merchant class in Yirmiyahu's time trusted that this story would be repeated, but to Yirmiyahu two factors in the current emergency must have appeared strikingly and appallingly different.

First, the king of a century earlier, unlike the current monarch, had been one who maintained programs caring for the city's poor and who outlawed religious practices of foreign origin.

Second, this time the dead were not outside but inside the walls. The living and the dead, both starving, were locked in together.

One personal note before we begin. The scrolls of Yirmiyahu are often treated as the first jeremiad, an outpouring of rage and gnashing of teeth against a city's injustice and decay. But there is a lake of emotion, cold and dark, beneath those quick bursts of anger. These scrolls are a lamentation (to me, a poignant one), a wrestling with the likelihood of despair. Historians know that the city fell after a bitter and protracted siege and that the few survivors were led away in chains, their temples looted and burned, their abandoned homes loud with the moans of the dead. Yirmiyahu's recorded sayings come to us as cries in the dark; pleas for justice that fell, at the time, on deaf or frightened ears. His story confronts us with the horror that our greatest efforts to heal and preserve our communities may not be enough. In the end, there may only be hunger, illness, and a slow death that brings neither peace nor rest.

The horror of what Yirmiyahu saw and what he endured is nearly too much for me. In reencountering his words, we can do one of two things. We can flinch away—turn our back on the suffering and eat, drink, and be merry, leaving death until tomorrow. Or we can gaze on the horror with unblinking eyes and listen with shuddering hearts, and make the choice Yirmiyahu demands, searching within ourselves or asking of God whether we have the courage to live lives of hope and action even when faced with almost certain failure, letting our efforts burn hot as a sun in a universe that appears governed (though we hope and trust that it isn't) only by the law of entropy.

FIRST DAY: TRUTH AT THE BOTTOM OF THE WELL

By the time they lowered Yirmiyahu into the old well behind the king's house, the city around them was already dying. Neither the king nor the priests would admit it, but there were more dead every day, and some of those dead were walking.

It was an empty well, nearly dry; yet when Yirmiyahu reached the bottom he found mud, and for a moment he panicked, his throat seizing up—he didn't know how deep the mud might be; his legs sank into it. Then there was solid earth under his feet. The mud was higher than his knees, a cold, wet suck around his legs. He shivered and shrank against one of the cistern's stone walls as the guards pulled the rope back up. He thought about clutching it, realized it would be useless. They would only lower him back in—or haul him halfway up and drop him, claiming an "accident."

The men above were laughing as they left; he could hear echoes of it, distorted in the long shaft of the well. He gazed up. A circle of sunlight, pale and distant, far above him, a reminder that somewhere above this hole in the ground there was light and deity. He lifted his hand, shaking a little. Even if he could not reach that light, he could perhaps be heard. "God!" he cried. "Help me out of here. Don't let me perish like this."

The echoes of the guards' mockery had faded, and no voice of God or man answered Yirmiyahu from that high circle. His heart quailed; he drew a shuddering breath and stilled the shaking of his hands.

Well. He was here.

He forced his gaze down. The mud lay quiet in these shadows unless he moved. He'd smuggled half a crust of bread into his loincloth—the only clothing they'd left him. His back and arms were scraped and sore from the times he had swung against the stones as they lowered him. His hair and beard had not been cut in long months, while he'd been locked in a cell in the cellar of the king's house; he must look like a nazarite, like Samson of old, who slew a thousand walking corpses with only a donkey's jawbone.

The stones against his back were cold so he stood in the middle for a while, his legs trembling. He'd almost forgotten how to stand in the last dark months. Closing his eyes, he felt the still air, listened, listened. He might yet hear God's voice again—he might hear her even in this dark well. He might. That silence above him was as terrifying as the darkness in which he stood—this clinging, tangible *hoshekh*, a darkness that touched both body and spirit. For once, no divine words welled up within him. Perhaps God had already turned away from the decaying city, and from Yirmiyahu within it.

He breathed, and listened, tried to slow the beating of his heart. Tried to remember how to think. He was a levite; though others of the priestly caste disowned him as a troublemaker and a rabble-rouser, he was still a levite, a dedicate; a levite must have the deepest commitment to God and to the Covenant (that he'd learned from his father) and to the People (that he'd learned from his wife). They might throw him in a well; still, he was a levite and a prophet. In the street or in a well, he would hold to his covenant with God.

He hungered but did not eat. He didn't know whether Zedekiah the king had ordered him into the well for only a day or for two days or three, or if he'd been left here to die. He didn't know how long he'd already stood here in the mud. He glanced up. The light above looked more pale than before. Besides that far circle, he saw where there was light on one side of the well below it; the sun had been above him when they lowered him into this place, but now it must have swung across the sky. I will know how many days pass, he thought. The chill was creeping inside him, making him shake. He might not last the night without clothing to cover him. Up there, the heat baked every hint of favor and life out of the city, but down here it was cold as dream country. His lips felt dry. "We are People of the Covenant," he whispered. "Each of us made in the likeness of God." He repeated it, words that comforted though they did not warm him. In the silence of God, Yirmiyahu murmured the words his God had given him before, words whispered to him in the dark, over the past few years. The words that mattered. "We are People of the Covenant. We are the spouse of our God."

He thought of the city, the heat making the air over its walls ripple. He thought of its quiet gardens with their dry beds where once there had been pools of quiet water, its stone paths, its treasure-houses. The palace of the king, with this deep well in one of its lower courtyards. And the crowded back streets, where Yirmiyahu had taken to living these past months, after sending his wife away from the city before the siege. These were the dry streets of an unreplenished city relying on dried or drying wells, where bands of orphans hunted for scraps or broke into smaller houses to tear food from the larders. He had seen a young child dying in one street, her skin stretched too tight over her ribs, her eyes wide and unseeing. In the next street, mothers who could still afford bread baked cakes for Astarte, the most popular of Yerusalem's foreign goddesses, and pretended they could not hear others' children begging for food at the door or crying in the night.

"I know your ways," he whispered, reciting the words God had found for him, words she'd sent, through him, to priests who didn't wish to hear. He trailed his fingers through the mud. It had been a season since he had felt the ground wet. There was a sheen of dirt over his body. "I know your ways. You've relied on broken and dried cisterns rather than the well that nourishes. God says: *You were my branches, beautiful with good fruit, well watered and tall. But drought will come with a roar from the desert, and the branches are withering.*"

How strange, this cold mud under his fingers, earth that had become full of water yet grew nothing. Yirmiyahu lifted his hand toward his eyes but could no longer see his fingers. Everything was dark. He looked up again. There were stars there, beautiful though faint, too far away to give him light. His stomach snarled like a lion, and he took the bread crust from his loincloth, lifted it to his mouth. It was hard and dry and had no flavor. It hurt his teeth to chew it; he thought of dipping it in the mud to moisten it, decided not to. He kept chewing slowly and at last swallowed a little bit of it. That made him thirsty, which was worse. He kept eating.

Something moved against his leg and he jumped, almost dropping the bread. With a sob he leaned back against the wall and finished the crust. Only a worm, or some snake. He was not alone in this mud, then; some other living creature God had birthed into the world was here with him. He tried to calm his breathing, take comfort from that. He looked at the stars again. Other people in the city, and in the land, were perhaps gazing up at those same remote stars. Even his wife might be standing at this moment at the door or the window of a house in the village he'd sent her back to, her face tilted up and bathed in starlight. Yirmiyahu moaned and leaned against the well's cold stones.

Up there, beneath those same stars, an army was camped about the city, keeping its people trapped inside the walls, in narrow streets between buildings of stone or dried mud with sun-baked white roofs; and, inside the walls where food and water were already short, the plague. A few unclean dead, or many (their number grew so fast), were hunting in the alleys. He thought of the shambling corpses, their hands scratching at doors, pulling at the fragile wood. A few months ago, he had seen two—one had been a priest, *a priest*, one of his own caste, still clad in the simple white robes of the levites who kept the Temple—he'd seen those two tear down a door and drag a woman out into the street. He had run at them, crushed one's head with a shovel he'd taken from a worker at the wall. But the other—the priest—had sunk its teeth deep into the woman's shoulder. He remembered her cry of pain, the wildness of her eyes, her terror. He remembered the way the walking corpse that fed on her looked up at him when he came at it, its eyes with nothing in them but hunger and animal hostility. He remembered its wavering moan.

After the priest lay unmoving in the dust, Yirmiyahu killed the woman. Gasping as he leaned over the shovel, gazing down at her broken body. No one else came. He had stood there a long time, shaking, gazing in horror at the woman he'd killed. The body would otherwise have risen to hunger and eat in the dark—yet this had been a woman's body, a sacred and life-giving body, shaped in the likeness of God herself. Yirmiyahu gazed at the woman's eyes, glazing already in death. It was too terrible for tears; he just stood and shook.

Now, in the well, he wrapped his arms around himself and stumbled in slow circles through the mud, trying to stay on his feet, trying to keep warm, though he was so weary, though in this darkness he felt as though his mind might come apart as easily as a bread crust soaked in mud. "We are the People of the Covenant," he said hoarsely in the dark, "each of us made in God's likeness." He kept saying it; it was good to hear words, though speaking made his throat more dry.

He had barely been a man when he first heard those words, newly come to Yerusalem from his father's village, a few short years past, with a small pack of white clothing and gifts from his grandmother, and a lovely and laughing wife walking beside him. He'd meant to study with the levites at the Temple; in fact, he had just secured his small house in the city with the coin his father had sent with him. He meant to go to see the priests at the Temple steps in the morning, the long lines of them with their austere faces.

Then God had spoken in a voice that made the hot night air tremble. Yirmiyahu had been dressed in a loincloth then, as now, for it had been the middle of the night. He'd stepped out of his new house into the street and listened, while Miriam dreamed in their bed. The stars had been as far away then as they were now, but all around him was the looming presence of the lives of the people of that new city, in their hundred stone houses.

Yirmiyahu, the voice called. *My Yirmiyahu.*

"Are you calling me, *adonai*?" he whispered.

There was a silence. Then the voice was at his ear. *Before you were in your mother's womb, I knew you.* The voice became a whisper, as though sharing a secret between the two of them. *Before you were born, I set you apart, called you as my* navi, *my prophet.*

That word rushed through Yirmiyahu like a sudden wind through the door of a house, knocking aside his carefully placed furniture and pulling curtains and veils aside from the openings to inner rooms. The *navi*, the prophet, the bringer of *niv sefatayim*, the fruit from God. There had been many in the history of the land, men and women who could hear God and who carried God's words to the People, words as full and round and fertile as fruit. There had been many, but Yirmiyahu didn't know of any who now spoke or did healing in the land. *Navi, navi*: he trembled.

"Yes, *adonai*," he breathed, his eyes wide. He knew there could be no other answer, not to the One who now spoke. He knelt, there in the street, his heart shaking within him. "But *adonai*, I am young, I am—"

There was a soft pressure against his lips—like a woman's fingers hushing him—a touch cool and soft, a touch of divine fingers. He trembled, his heart beating within the well of his chest. All about him in the air, he sensed God quivering, vitally present, like a vast tree invisible in the night, a deep and inexhaustible well beneath its roots, water drawn upward, cool and quiet, to the full fruit that clung to all God's branches.

Do not go to the priests in the morning, the voice said, and the invisible branches moved gently in the air. *Go to the people, my* navi. *Look in the streets, look at how my People live, how they keep the Covenant, see what they do in this city. Then, when it is nearly dusk and wind is in the olives, go to the priests. Take my words, Yirmiyahu. Take them to the Temple. I have set you this day against those who lead nations and cities, to pluck up and to break down, to destroy and to overthrow, to build and to plant. Go, Yirmiyahu.* That small, small whisper in his ear, soft as wind in trees yet firm with command. *Prepare yourself. Take my words and speak them. I make you this day a fortified city, a rooted cedar, a wall. They will fight against you, my* navi, *they will throw themselves against you, but they will not prevail against you, for I am with you, to keep you and deliver you, nourish you and strengthen you.*

A rustle above him broke his thoughts as abruptly as a man breaks a twig; glancing up, Yirmiyahu saw shapes silhouetted coldly against the stars. He called hoarsely for help, heard an echo of laughter again. His tormentors were back. They threw something out over that hole of sky, and it fell. For an instant his heart surged with hope at the thought of food, a bundle of food; then he felt the rush of air and the mass of it hit the mud beside him in the terrible dark. He heard the cracking of bone, and his belly heaved at the sweet and overpowering stench of the rotting dead. The thing stirred, and he saw two glints of starlight—eyes in the dark. A low, shuddering moan filled his ears, surrounding him, echoing in the narrow well.

With a cry, Yirmiyahu lurched back. Stumbling, he fell into the mud. Kicking out with his feet, he scrambled away until he felt the stone wall cold against his shoulders.

The glints of light were coming toward him. A loud slurping of mud as the thing moved, dragging its broken body through the muck. The creature's moan went on and on. He could not see it in the dark, but he knew it was reaching for him, fingers groping in the dark to seize his leg and pull him toward its teeth. He kept kicking, his heart wild with beating, his breath coming fast. Light-headed with fear. He felt the brush of its fingertips against his skin and shuddered with loathing, as though maggots had touched him in the mud. With a low cry he got his knees under him, the mud cool around his thighs; reaching down, he seized the creature's hair in its fingers, seized the hair near the roots and hauled the thing's head away from his leg. It hissed and twisted, trying to bite at his arm; its strength was terrible. With his other hand he snatched his loincloth from about his hips, wadded it swiftly, and shoved it into the creature's mouth, muffling its low growl.

Yirmiyahu grasped its hair in both hands and forced its head down into the mud. His chest heaved as he panted and wheezed, his arms straining, his muscles screaming with the effort of holding down the corpse. Though the mud closing over its head silenced it, it did not grow still, nor did its limbs flail in panic. It was not a living man. It was an incarnation of raw hunger and need, and it required no air to live; its hands were beneath it, pushing. The creature strained to force its reeking body out of the mud, even as Yirmiyahu strained to keep it submerged. With a gasp of panic, Yirmiyahu felt his arms trembling; in another moment or two they would give out, and the hungering creature would be on him. Leaning his back against the wall for leverage, he lifted his leg with a wild shriek and brought his heel slamming down on the thing's head.

The blow pressed the thing deeper into the mud, but still it strained to rise. Screaming, Yirmiyahu brought his heel down again and again, with all the force he could, hard blows to the back of the thing's head. For a few moments, it kept fighting him; then Yirmiyahu felt something hard give beneath his heel, and the thing went limp. He smashed his heel into it twice more before falling back against the wall, moaning with horror. Before him in the dark, he saw the lumpy shape of the corpse's back above the mud. Yirmiyahu slammed his palms wildly against the stone wall at his sides, screaming through clenched teeth, trying to control his panic.

Dimly, he heard laughter somewhere far above him.

That sobered him. He fell silent, simply leaned against the wall, breathing hard. He didn't bother to look up; he didn't care to see the silhouettes of his tormenters leaning in, looking down into the dark, mocking his fight for survival. He growled low in his throat, anger bubbling on the rim of his mind. What people were they up there, joying in the torment of their prisoner? How could *these* be People of the Covenant, people who shared his city and his God?

His heart began to slow down. He dragged his hand across his eyes, wiping away dirt and muck and sweat. The laughter had stopped; one of them called down something, but the echoes of the well distorted the words. He did not plan to beg them for water or food, or even let them know whether he'd been bitten or not; doubtless they would grow bored in a few moments and go their way. His anger started to fade as fatigue crept over him again. They tormented him, he realized, because they were men without hope for the future. They grabbed at what small-hearted pleasures they could, because they were increasingly certain, somewhere deep in their spirit, that the next morning, or the morning after that, or some morning soon would find them cold and dead—or perhaps lurching, mindless, through a deserted city in search of meat. They had chosen not to hope.

He began to think, using this moment of cold clarity to hold off his fatigue and horror.

His loincloth was likely irrecoverable—but he could not last this night naked. He was certain of that. Hissing through his teeth, he bent quickly to do what had to be done. Shaking, he began stripping the creature of its clothes, fighting not to retch at the scent, muttering a Hebrew psalm under his breath—one of David's—to distract his mind from what he was doing. He could feel the thing's cold skin beneath his hands, not hard but terribly soft. He gagged, leaned into the wall a moment, fought for air. That touch—that *touch*—on his hands. On his heel, on his shin. He moaned. Unclean. He was unclean. He was a levite, and his hands had touched *the dead*. The words of the Covenant and the Law rang within him, demanding atonement, words of purpose and command that had been established centuries past, when the People were still tent dwellers in the desert, lying awake in their wool bedding and listening for the moan of the dead in the hills:

> You shall bury the flesh of the dead, and raise above it a cairn of stones, a warning to any that see.

> You shall not touch the flesh of the dead, for the dead body
> is unclean. If a man touches the flesh of the dead, you shall
> put him from your camp, and watch him. Seven days you
> shall put him from your camp.

Those were *mitzvot*, commandments for keeping the People clean
and vital and free of the clinging, hungering dead. Yirmiyahu's
palms stung where his fingernails dug into his skin.

He drew in ragged breaths. Unclean. He should be cast from
the People. He had touched the dead. Yet—he was already cast
out, already isolated. He glanced up at that circle high above him,
with its faint promise of starlight. He was in the dark, he was
alone, he was cold; he might well be left here the seven days that
the Covenant required for the cleansing of flesh that had touched
the dead, and his uncleanness in this well would harm no others
of the People. Unclenching his hands, he returned to his work.
He would *not* die here. He had been called to God's service, and
there *was* still a city to preserve, to call back to its Covenant.

He'd seen so many broken covenants. The priesthood had
broken faith with the people, hoarding grain while children
starved in the streets and condoning the defilements at Tophet.
The king had broken covenant with the people, delighting in
wealth rather than in the health and feeding of the city. The people themselves had broken covenant, binding themselves to other
deities, who demanded less and promised more than they could
indeed offer. Yirmiyahu hissed through his teeth as he peeled
cloth away from flesh. Even *he* had broken covenant—with his
wife. He'd sent Miriam away as the city grew violent. He squeezed
his eyes shut against the anguish of that memory.

But clean or unclean, he would not break covenant with God.
He was God's prophet, her *navi*: His task was to speak for her,
to gather her fruitful words and bring them, bring that water-
rich fruit to a people who insisted they were content with dried

crusts. He must do that; he must stay ready to do that, whatever came; he must last the night. He must keep trying. He had been thrown in here, unwilling to be silent; if the king ever let him out, he would not be silent then. But first he must live. The rhythmic phrases of the old Hebrew prayer soared from his lips, the prayer of David, louder and still louder, until the sound of his voice filled the well. Lifting one of the corpse's arms, he pulled its tunic free, then dropped the naked arm into the sucking mud and staggered back. The fabric he clutched was torn and filthy with blood and viscous fluid and muck; but if he could make it through this night, the next day might dry it. The tunic might be unclean, but it was clothing, it was life. Growling, he wrung out what dampness he could, then draped it over his shoulders. It was not warm but it was heavy, and perhaps that would make some difference.

———

For a while then he sank to his knees, the mud around his waist, and he shivered in his improvised shawl, fitfully moving from sleep to quiet sobbing, and back to sleep again. He woke in starts from half dreams in which he had felt the cutting of teeth into his arm or his leg. He woke with sharp, desperate cries, certain the corpse had risen from the mud, that it was groping for him. He tried to force himself to move, to reach for it and feel whether it lay still, there in the dark. He reached out his trembling hand, felt cold flesh, jerked it back. He was sweating. His hands kept shaking. He tried to reach out again, but he couldn't, he couldn't. It was coming for him, it was coming in the dark. He shrank against the wall and listened, listened for that terrible moan. Heard only his quick heartbeats. Shaking. Unable to sleep, he knelt sobbing, leaning his back against the wall, his own wrenching, human moans repeating one word, the name of his wife. Over half a year since he'd seen her. "Miriam," he groaned, "Miriam. Miriam—"

Muttering without cease, he called the darkness by its name: *hoshekh*. Naming it, knowing it, might at least keep it from choking him: *hoshekh*. The darkness that is darkest of all darknesses, the darkness that hides in the back of caves. The darkness that fills the mind of one who refuses to hear the cries in the street, the darkness that hides behind the ribs of a man or a woman, that eats at everything that is real and true inside them. *Hoshekh*. Once, the Lawgiver had called a plague of *hoshekh* upon the people of the cities of the Nile, who had not heard the cries of their slave workers or their wives, the cries when soldiers took their infants and drowned them in the river. And when those unhearing people yawned and lay themselves down for sleep, the *hoshekh* poured from their mouths like dark milk until their houses and their land was filled with it. When they woke in the morning, they were blind and could not even move from their beds, for the *hoshekh* was heavy on them as they lay, and heavy inside them, as though they were at the bottom of a pool of dark mud. For three days and three nights they lay moaning in the *hoshekh*, while the people of Israel ate and sang in the hovels of the slave encampments, where there was light and, for once, no work.

Hoshekh, Yirmiyahu called this darkness in the well that pressed on his skin. The whole city above must be filled with it, this night. Darker than dark, the city. Only the dead could move through it with their slow feet, their leaning bodies scraping against the walls of houses and shops, their fingers reaching over the stone, hungering.

——

When he opened his eyes, it was still dark. He did not know whether it was the same night or another, or how long he'd slept. His stomach growled like a wild beast fighting to gnaw open his belly. He trembled in his rags and cried out wordlessly. He passed his hand over his face, saw only its outline. His lips were terribly dry, his tongue and throat more so. The stench of death in the well was strong, still too strong to become used to, and he retched into the mud in great heaves, though little came up, for he had already retched up the bread and water he had in him. He was still on his knees, and when he moved them a little he found his legs were numb and stiff; when he moved them a little more, they went violent with pain. Clenching his teeth, he waited for the pain to pass. Tears ran from the corners of his eyes, hot against his cheeks.

He had awakened from an evil dream; frayed tatters of it still clung to him like the clothes he wore, clothes he'd taken from the dead. Waking, he still saw the faces of children, the whites around their eyes, heard the shrieks from their open mouths. Saw the rotting flesh of the hands that gripped them, pulling them down into the pit. Standing in a circle about the pit, men and women with pale faces and their arms at their sides. The pit atop the hill of Tophet. In his dream he screamed at them. "I see the blood of children on your skirts!" he cried, extending his arms toward the women, but he couldn't reach them.

For just one moment, he thought maybe—maybe—that hill, all of it, had been only a dream. Maybe it had only ever been night terrors and nothing more. Maybe he had dreamed it all, here at the bottom of this cold well. But no: it had been real, terribly real.

———

In the tense months before the siege began, Yirmiyahu had still lived with Miriam his wife in their little house near the gates of the city. It had been his habit in the afternoons to urge the men at the city gates to petition the priests for bread and grain to feed Yerusalem's forgotten children; many times he'd lifted his eyes to the hill while he spoke and seen the haze of smoke above its ridge. From the position of the smoke in the hot air, Yirmiyahu could tell that it came from the old shrine on the hill's far slope—a sign that some of the People had resumed sacrifices to Chemosh, the heathen god who lived at the shrine. Sometimes Yirmiyahu would fall silent in the midst of a heated conversation with a merchant at the gates and stare for a long time at that smoke. Eventually the merchant would turn to look, too. Some of the merchants scowled then and made a sign against evil with their fingers; others took on a thoughtful look. Other times the merchant's face would darken with shame, and he'd turn quickly and strike up a conversation with some other man who was near, eager for a reason to hide his face from the *navi*.

The hill troubled Yirmiyahu. For the *navi*, monotheism was a fiercely ethical matter, in a way that later men in later centuries would rarely understand or remember. To Yirmiyahu's mind, being covenanted to one woman and to one God taught a man steadiness, the steadiness needed to stand in a strong wind. To have many women or many deities was to be buffeted by winds from many directions; it meant not knowing who one was called upon to protect and worship. It meant being accustomed to a degree of faithlessness, to offering merely a conditional devotion to both God and woman. It meant the ease of distraction, of picking and choosing from one's responsibilities and relationships, laying down those that were most difficult at a particular moment and devoting more of oneself instead to those that required less work and less truth.

Other tribes saw these things differently, quite differently, but Yirmiyahu was the descendant of generations of levites, and he was watching the city of his People die. His unease with seductive, heathen deities was hot in his chest. Gazing at the smoke on the hill's summit, Yirmiyahu almost thought he could hear, faint in the day's heat, the calling of those hungry gods and goddesses whom his People had not brought with them out of the desert long ago but had found waiting for them in this land. Deities who spread their arms wide and moaned: *Come to me, I will give you wealth or security or love, or what you desire, only feed me, feed me. I am so hungry; don't you want to feed me?*

Sometimes, as Yirmiyahu looked up at that smoke, the cries of those other gods, who had established no abiding Covenant with the People, rose from a faint moan on the hill to a shriek of urgent, demanding need; at those times he would look away from the summit, shivering even in the heat of day as the merchants at the gate chattered and argued around him. And all the while, Yirmiyahu's God murmured from behind the veil in her Temple, *I am here. If you want me, you must be faithful to me, and you must nourish my children. You must work hard to provide for them. Then I will let you take me in your arms and I will delight you and nourish you.* A God of Covenant for a People of the Covenant, a divine spouse rather than a divine lover. That is how the *navi* saw it.

It would be an easy thing, perhaps, to keep his eyes from straying to that hill. To not ask what sacrifices Chemosh received up there. Yet Yirmiyahu couldn't stop looking. The sight of that haze gnawed at him. Of all the People's lovers, he *feared* Chemosh. Chemosh was a god apart. Astarte's love was playful and vitalizing; Baal's was stern and demanding; Dagon's was tempestuous, overwhelming, and fickle as the sea in which he swam with his fish; but Chemosh—that was a god who would beat his lovers and batter them. And Chemosh would only grin darkly in the knowledge that such treatment would just convince his worshippers all the more of his power and his strength to provide for them, keep them, and shield them: that the more he beat his worshippers, the more they would fall to the earth, kiss his feet, and beg for the privilege of feeding him.

In bed at night, with the soft breathing of his wife beside him, Yirmiyahu would wake sometimes, thinking of that hill, trying to persuade himself that those sons and daughters of the People who visited the shrine were bringing only fruit or sheaves of barley to the god. Yet his heart told him it wasn't so.

Once he came awake with a start, thinking he'd heard weeping. He bolted upright and gazed into the dark, but the sound faded from hearing as swiftly as any dream sound might. Miriam stirred beside him. "What is it, husband?" Her voice heavy with sleep.

Yirmiyahu was breathing hard, the sheets sweaty beneath him. He didn't look at her; he kept gazing in the direction from which the sound had come, if there had actually been a sound. His ears strained to hear it. With a dryness in his throat, he realized he was staring in the direction of the Temple.

"Yirmiyahu?" A little fear in her voice. There were dead now in some of the alleys of the city. A noise in the night was something to fear.

Yirmiyahu let out his breath slowly. He didn't wish to frighten her with what was likely only a dream. Turning to her, he saw her eyes soft and liquid in the dark. Her soft form on the bed caught at his heart; he set his hand on her thigh.

"A bad dream," he murmured.

After a moment he felt her small hands take his, drawing his palm to her lips. He let his heartbeat slow; if God was weeping for something done on that hill—if she needed him—she would call for him. But right now his wife needed him. This had not been an easy year for her, and she was more often the one who woke with bad dreams. The moist warmth of her lips pressed his hand, and he tried to smile in the dark but couldn't. Couldn't shake the feeling that something was terribly, terribly wrong.

"Come back to sleep," Miriam whispered.

He lay beside her and took her firmly in his arms, feeling the warmth of her; the hard bite of his anxiety eased.

Miriam pressed herself to him, kissing his neck once, and stroked his back with her fingers. After a while her hands slowed and were still; her breathing slowed. He kissed her hair and held her, wakeful, while she slept. He kept listening in the dark, waiting to hear that sound of weeping a second time.

Yirmiyahu didn't close his eyes again that night.

———

God did call for him—the next day.

As noon approached and Yirmiyahu wended through the narrow streets toward the gates, God whispered to him. There was pleading in her voice. *There are things I need you to see,* she whispered. *There are things you need to know, my* navi. *Up on the hill. Go to the hill, my* navi.

If he had known just how terrible those things would be, what God would ask him to endure, perhaps he wouldn't have had the courage to climb that hill. As it was, Yirmiyahu climbed slowly, reluctantly. He glanced over his shoulder once at the roofs of the city within its walls, wooden roofs and roofs of brick clay, mixed patches of bright and dark in the afternoon glare of the sun. Then, turning his back, he went to see what it was that he must see, a grimness in his face. He met no one else on the slope; whatever worshippers had been here were not here now. It was a long climb, and when he reached the summit under its brooding oaks, he was nearly out of breath.

There he found the altar, and behind it, the massive statue of the god, a thing of gold under the trees. Yirmiyahu's eyes took in its distended belly, its bloated, grasping hands, its gaping mouth. The god's lower jaw hung down to its feet, and through it, Yirmiyahu could see the sacrificial pit, a hole opened in the earth. On the god's golden lips—the lips of the pit—Yirmiyahu could see stains. He shrank back, turned from the pit a moment to touch the ashes on the altar. Still warm. And two great lamps yet burned at either side of the god, their oil sending up a heavy-scented smoke.

He swallowed. Some of the People had been here, feeding the god, even earlier that very day, though they were now gone. He glanced again at the god's face. Chemosh's eyes were small, just tiny notches in the gold statue, and Yirmiyahu did not feel watched. The god was fed, content, and in any case this was not a god of seeing or hearing. This god was all mouth and belly.

Who had been here, feeding it? Olive farmers from the slopes of the Mount on the other side of the city, where olive trees, beloved of the People, swayed in the wind? Or tanners and potters and anxious craftsmen come out from within the city walls? What people were feeding this god? And what was the god eating? A levite who had been raised hearing all the lore of his People, Yirmiyahu knew enough about the hungers of the heathen gods for horror to paralyze his heart. Seeing those stains on the golden lips, he could hardly breathe.

Get a torch. The voice of his own God came in a whisper through the leaves overhead. *See what your own People, my People, are doing.*

Yirmiyahu refused for a moment, hanging back, dread chilling his body.

Get a torch, my navi. The voice in the air was insistent.

Yirmiyahu cast about, found a fallen oak branch, gasped even as he reached for it—for there, caught on a jagged root of the oak, a tattered strip of white wool lay dirtied on the earth. No doubt it had been torn loose from the hem of someone's garment. The sight of it tore through Yirmiyahu. He crouched, touched the wool gently, lifted a bit of it between his fingers. He began to tremble. The oak had torn this wool from a *levite*'s garment; he was certain of it. The weave was fine, and his fingers could detect the pattern that was woven into the hems of the robes worn by every male of the priestly caste. His own hem was woven in the same pattern. His hand shook, and he fell back on his rear, breathing hard.

A levite had been here. His heart grappled with this; perhaps the priest had come only as he himself had, to spy out the doings on the hill. Perhaps it had only been that. But the cold horror that gripped him, tightening his throat, told him otherwise. The levite had been here as a participant. With irrevocable and wrenching certainty, Yirmiyahu *knew* this.

Getting to his feet and returning, shaking, to the altar, he lit the branch he carried from one of the lamps. He lifted the branch high over the pit, dread closing his throat; a circle of firelight lit the earthen floor below—a floor near enough to leap down but too far to climb back. There were bones there, many of them. Small ones, so small, the bones of children of the People—femurs and ribs, and at least two skulls within the reach of the torchlight. And that stench, rising from the bowels of the god. The horror licked at the bottom of his throat, bile rising in him. He covered his mouth and nose with his hand and kept looking, feeling the presence of his God at his shoulders, like a great terebinth with her branches leaning over him, shading him.

The whisper of God's voice came to him, soft yet irresistible as wind in the branches. *My People try to drink from dried and broken cisterns*, the voice whispered, *and forsake the well that nourishes; they forsake me. Instead of replenishment, desiccation. Instead of birth and growth, the withering of the young. Instead of my womb, this grave in a god's belly.*

Yirmiyahu peered down at the bones in the flickering light. The reek dismayed him, and the nearness of the god's statue dismayed him, too. Those bones, bits of digested people in the god's belly, made him cry out without sound, his mouth open, his insides heaving. He retched at the lip of the pit.

Long ago his own ancestors had sacrificed their firstborn at altars, even as other peoples in the farther parts of the land still did. But one of his People's oldest stories told of the Akedah, the binding of the firstborn, when God had placed her hand at Abraham's chest and stopped him from drawing his knife across his son's throat. When Yirmiyahu had been a small boy, his father had told the tale with horror and panache, and young Yirmiyahu had shivered to think of the upraised hand, the flash of the knife, the cry of the boy.

Abraham had taught this to all his children, and they to their children: We do not feed God, God feeds us. God is sufficient to feed herself and us. To honor her, give back some of the food she has given—fruit of the orchard or the first of the flock—but do not give your own young, for that is an abomination before God who brings all births.

Now Yirmiyahu gazed down into the foreign god's dark belly, and his insides became cold. He wondered how many of the People had come to worship here, how many had come to feed the god. Was it easier to covenant with a god you'd fed, one you hoped would owe you gratitude, however cruel that god might be, than it was to covenant with a God who fed you?

He stared down at the bones. As the initial bite of his horror dulled (though the stench of the pit remained intense), he tried to understand those remains. Some of the bones were cracked, as though a great beast had broken them to suck out the marrow. A fresh chill took Yirmiyahu. Gods did not need to break bones to feed. Something mortal had *fed* on those children the People had tossed into the god's belly.

The need to understand this horror—the need to know, to see what his God wanted him to witness—that need steeled his heart and limbs. He stared down at those bones in the torchlight, thinking quickly of how he might make a rope—perhaps tearing up his own robe and braiding the strips—to get down there for a closer look. There were just those bones and their terrible riddle, down there. Nothing else. He waited a long moment, trying not to retch. Then—then—

A shambling, leaning figure lurched across the circle of light below. A small figure, no larger than a boy of eight, its head turned to the ground, unaware of the watcher above it. Moving slowly, dragging one leg, but without any apparent pain. It simply limped across his view and disappeared again into the dark beyond the torch's reach.

With a sharp gasp, Yirmiyahu flung himself back, away from the pit, falling onto his side in the twigs and leaves beneath the oaks. His torch, fallen, clattered over the lip of the hole and disappeared. A breath afterward, a long, low wail from beneath the earth. A shuddering moan. Even the oak branches above appeared to tremble at it. Yirmiyahu threw an arm across his eyes and pressed himself to the earth, unable to breathe. His entire body tensed in wild denial.

The moan faltered. There were a few more after it, several together. There were dead in the pit: walking, hungering dead. He felt the scream building inside him, a scream that caught behind his tonsils and would not come out, would never come out. He felt like choking.

Perhaps one of the dead had fallen into the pit, then fed on the children who were brought to the god—children who then rose to moan and stumble about the pit themselves. Or perhaps one of the child sacrifices had been bitten before the child was brought to the hill, the bite concealed beneath a ceremonial vesture so that the child's parents might not be dishonored or declared unclean. Perhaps that child had been feverish when brought to the altar and had risen afterward in the earth—to feed later on the other sacrifices. Whatever horror had occurred, the pit was now full of the unclean dead.

The thought struck Yirmiyahu with a clarity as bracing and impossible to ignore as ice water poured, stabbing, at his face. The People, his People, his God's People, were not on this hill feeding Chemosh, eater of children and protector of cities; they were feeding *the dead*. The unburied dead.

He couldn't understand this.

It bewildered him and tore at him and shattered him; he lay on the ground shaking.

He lay there through most of the evening, caught between panic and prayer, tossing in a sickness that was not of the body. A wind stirred the oak leaves above, and there was a quiet creaking of branches. Sometimes, in it, he heard the soothing whispers of his God. Whenever the wind was still he could smell the dead, and he waited for the wind to come back.

———

Returning to the city before dusk, Yirmiyahu strode in wrath to the levites' houses in the street of the Temple. He burst into the home of the high priest, shattering the door from its jamb, as furious in his need to get in as though he himself were one of the dead. A woman inside had been slicing roots with an iron knife; now she shrieked at the apparition of this man in priestly robes with his hair flying and his eyes hot with rage.

At the breaking of the door and the scream, the high priest came from the back room, in his prayer shawl. Yirmiyahu seized him by the throat and slammed him into the wall; the priest was not a small man, but Yirmiyahu's speed and ferocity shocked him into paralysis.

"*What have you done?*" Yirmiyahu roared.

"What?" the priest gasped. "What?"

"You are the head of our caste in the city, you *must* know about it! What have you done on Tophet?"

The priest's eyes glanced to the side.

"Don't." Yirmiyahu squeezed slightly, his chest heaving. "Truth, I want truth."

The priest wetted his lips; his hand clutched Yirmiyahu's wrist, but the *navi* did not let him go.

"The People believe if we feed the dead—" The priest's voice was hoarse from the prophet's grip on his throat; "—they will not hunger so much for us. Then they can perhaps rest again."

The words speared Yirmiyahu. Now it was clear—the moaning in the pit, the bones of children, all clear. All terribly clear. Even as a few dead moaned within the walls of the city, the dead now moaned within the enclosure of the pit. The People were tossing a few of their firstborn into the pit at Tophet to suffer there in place of their other children, those they prayed would now be safe in the streets of their city, the hunger of the dead abated and mollified.

Yirmiyahu stared at this priest, the high priest of the People, as at some animal that had lifted up onto two legs and drawn about itself the skin of a man. Always before, in Yirmiyahu's crying out of God's words on the Temple steps, he'd thought the high priest a familiar, comprehensible thing, a priest drunk with comfort and prestige, neglectful of People and Covenant. But now the priest seemed to Yirmiyahu's eyes not merely something far worse but also something unexpected and alien. Yirmiyahu found it difficult to breathe.

"Abomination," Yirmiyahu snarled. "This is *not* how we serve God in Anathoth."

"You're not *in* Anathoth." The priest's eyes were dark.

Yirmiyahu stood panting, his hand still gripping the priest's throat, holding him to the wall but without squeezing. He felt eyes on his back—the woman who had been cutting roots. Suddenly he felt closed in, locked in this house with mad people. "I will make sure *every* levite knows about this," he hissed.

"Most of them know already," the priest said.

Yirmiyahu could see the truth of it in the priest's eyes, hear it in his own ears. In his heart, he reeled. The levites of the city were defiled! The caste was defiled: it had broken Covenant. The very robes Yirmiyahu wore on his body were defiled. "Unclean," he hissed, his hand trembling at the man's throat, everything in him shaking, wanting for one wild instant to squeeze and cut off the other man's breath. "Unclean!"

"You are a fool, Yirmiyahu," the priest rasped, his throat moving beneath Yirmiyahu's hand. "A fool who thinks he hears God. God stopped speaking to us generations ago. God no longer hears; God has left the land, and I do not believe there is any *navi*. The Ark is empty. What is important now is to keep the People calm, make them unafraid. King and People tithe to the Temple and know they will have peace from living enemies. And they bring offerings to Chemosh on his hill, knowing they will have peace from the dead. Why should we object to what happens on that hill? Going there, people don't have to be afraid. These are small sacrifices, young man."

"I will *find* someone to tell," Yirmiyahu roared.

"Do that," the priest wheezed. "Spit on your own caste, if you will. Just get out of my house."

"I will *raise* this city against you!" Yirmiyahu hissed. He threw the man to the floor and stood over him, his chest heaving; the woman watching from the other room screamed and came at him with the knife, but Yirmiyahu dodged it and then rushed out the broken door and into the street. There was a cry behind him but no pursuit; he ran wildly through the streets, hurrying toward the small house where he lived with Miriam. As he ran, he tore the robes from his back and dropped them into the dust, until he was bolting through the night street in his loincloth, his hair streaming behind him. Window slats clacked shut as he passed. His side burned, but he didn't slow; he had to run, he had to run, or he would collapse crying again in the dust.

———

From that day, Yirmiyahu wore no wool that had the patterns of his caste woven into it. Those patterns had been defiled and he could not wear them, not until the caste was redeemed, the tomb at Tophet filled with earth, and the city fed and healed. Instead he took up the brown garments of a common day laborer each morning, then went to the Temple to cry out the words God had whispered to his heart when he rose at dawn from the bed he shared with his wife.

"I know your ways!" he shouted on the wide Temple steps to a gathering crowd of levites in their white robes, merchants in their red robes, a few laborers in brown, and, in the back of the crowd, a few veiled women in the shade of the sunbaked brick houses of the priests that lined both sides of the street. Many of the priests frowned darkly; some of the merchants looked pale with fear. Some were listening, some looked troubled.

Sometimes as Yirmiyahu spoke a shudder would pass through the crowd, as though a cold wind had swept down the street. None of them spoke or murmured or whispered while the prophet pleaded with them, this man who said he was a *navi*, his voice sharp in the silence, echoing from the walls of the priests' houses. His listeners were tense; he knew that even those whose faces did not show it held fear clutched in their breasts. All the city was tense. There were rumors of trouble with Babylon, bad trouble, perhaps even an army on the way. A siege might mean a long time without wares coming or going from the markets. Those merchants in the crowd, when they walked to the city gates to converse with other men of trade, had only to glance up to see the armed men the king had paid to stand on the walls of the city. So most of them did not look up when they went to the gates.

And all they had to do was glance down the back streets as they passed by to see the hunger of the city's poor and to hear, from time to time, a moan from one of the city's dead, hungering and eating in the city's narrowest, darkest streets. So most of them did not look down those alleys.

"These are the words I bring you from God!" Yirmiyahu cried. Though he had stood twice a week on these steps since coming to the city, today his eyes were dark with the knowledge of what he'd seen on high Tophet. He spoke with more suffering and fury than he ever had before. "God says: *I know your ways! You say to each other, Peace, there will be peace, for look! The Temple, the Temple of God, the Temple of God is here! All of you are deceived.*"

His nostrils flared—it seemed to Yirmiyahu in that moment that a reek of decay was rising from the street, the same reek he had smelled above the pit on the hill. It was thick; it nauseated him. Even his own skin stank of it. "There is no peace, do not *talk* about peace!" he cried. "We are People of *the Covenant*! If the least of us falls on the desert road, we are to turn back and lift him onto our shoulders before we walk on. If any women hunger in the field, we are to leave some food behind for them to glean. Yet in our city, this very city where our God consents to dwell with us, you don't look outside your windows. You hear the scream of a woman violated in the alley and you cover your ears. No man is taken and stoned for that defilement. You hear a child crying from an empty belly and you go to your inner room and eat, humming to yourself to shut out the noise. You don't look outside your windows. And now death, death has come up into our windows! Why can't you hear it? Our pact with God is rent and torn, a rending made terribly visible to us in the tearing of flesh in the teeth of the unclean dead." He raged now, and the merchants' faces were white. Yet the priests listened with dark, furious faces; he met their eyes, screaming out his words, challenging them, demanding that they respond, that they act. What veil did they wear over their eyes? How could the city's suffering and peril be so hidden from the eyes of these sightless men?

"Levites!" he cried. "Men of my caste! How can you wear those garments? God's garments, given to our father's fathers when they vowed to bring the suffering of the People before God and bring God's mercy and nurturing back to her People. To reach one hand to our God and with the other lift our People from the dirt—that is our calling! You care only for collecting tithes, and keeping the People quiet and unafraid. They should *be* afraid! Don't you understand that the things we do here will drive God from the city?

"How dare you come to this Temple in those garments! How can you not stand naked before us today, forbearing such clothing while any one of our People in the city is naked? For every woman and child stripped in some street or alcove of this city, God in whose likeness they were born is stripped and bruised. For every child taken up the hill to the pit, you throw God, too, into the hole. You stand by while she is defiled and beaten and thrown to the dust, and you stand here about these steps wearing her clothes! Hooting like owls in the ruins of this covenanted city: Peace, peace, we have peace! We have God's clothing; we wrap ourselves in it and look holy. We have God's Temple; we dwell in God's house that we've taken. We are satisfied. We have everything we want from God; let her cry in the street, for we have what we want from her. We are secure. We are safe. We have peace." Yirmiyahu screamed: "*What is this peace?*"

That was when one of them—he did not see who—hefted a rock from the dusty ground and hurled it at him. Other stones soon followed, hard and brutal.

———

Fear is a sickness.

To treat it, Yirmiyahu kept wandering alone and unsteady through the wide streets of his memory, only sometimes noticing the reek of the corpse or the wet, clammy mud around his legs. It was still dark at the bottom of the well, but he could sense the lumpy shape of the dead body rotting beside him in the mud. His feet were swollen and numb, his tongue large inside his dry mouth. He rested against the wall and had conversations with people who weren't there, though his lips barely moved.

Sometimes, smelling the dead in the well, he thought he was smelling the decay from the pit on Tophet. He shuddered in the dark. Once he pressed clenched fists to his temples and moaned.

His own efforts at the gates and at the Temple steps had not stopped the smoke from rising above that hill. After his flight through the streets, pelted by stones, and after sending his wife safely from the city the next day, Yirmiyahu had begun talking with the guardsmen of the walls, the younger ones, hoping to recruit some of them for a raid on the summit. If his cries at the Temple could not put an end to the sacrifices, perhaps a few swords might suffice. He was desperate; the anguish of what he had seen clutched at him, making it difficult to breathe when he thought of it.

Most of the guardsmen wouldn't listen to him, some because they were afraid of the priests. Others because there was no threat to their own children, and they did not want to see the need. Still others because they had seen dead in the streets and the heathen way of appeasement appealed to their minds. But a few were beginning to hear him, he thought.

Three weeks passed. Then one morning, even as the sun rose over the wall, something happened that drove Tophet utterly from his mind.

Yirmiyahu woke to the sound of clinking metal and shouts from the wall. When he wrapped a brown cloak about himself and stepped out into the street, people were screaming; there were many, many people in the streets, the olive farmers from the Mount and the barley farmers from the river valley, all rushing into the city. "They're shutting the gates!" the refugees cried. "The king's men are shutting the gates!"

Babylon had come.

Yirmiyahu stood on the edge of the street by the gate as the people streamed past, his hair lank and unwashed about his face, and terror took hold of his heart and squeezed it, so that he sank back against the wall of a house. A vision filled his mind, sights of what might be, of what evils the actions of this day might bring. Terrible images of the restless dead gnawing on bodies, many, many of them in the streets. Then God's words came, rushing wildly through him, a river, a torrent, a flash flood of speech, of warning and outcry. He screamed the words, right where he stood, even as the people flowed past.

At last he stepped out into the middle of the street, fighting the people who buffeted him, clawing his way toward the city's main gates, screaming in a fever of horror, desperate to be heard by the king's men, the armed men slamming heavy beams across the gates. "Death, death has come up into our windows!" he cried, as he tried in vain to force his way through the crowd. "We must yield the city! We must yield the city! Or the horses of the east will trample beneath their hooves only the bones of the dead! Open the gates! *Open the gates!* Do not lock the People in with the dead! Do not do this thing! God will leave the city! She'll flee the city!"

The siege shut about the city; small camps of tents sprung up to watch each of its gates, the sun bright on so many helmets and shields. Bowmen moved in and out of the tents and their horses whickered, so many horses, more perhaps than the land had ever seen. In the city for long months, people hungered while the priests rationed out grain to those who could afford it. There were famished, slouching dead in so many streets and ill-lit corners. Yirmiyahu heard their moaning through the boarded-up windows of the scribe's shop where he'd taken to living, having sold the house where he'd lived with his wife as soon as he sent her away.

There was rarely a day during the siege when Yirmiyahu could hold silence for long; the words came so fast and so forcefully that he was like a twig in a river. It was as though God was weeping behind her veil in the Temple, rocking in sorrow over the Ark while the dead ate in the streets. Wherever Yirmiyahu stood in the city he could hear her. In the scribe's shop, he would stir at times from a trancelike state to find that he'd been spilling God's mourning, desperate words from his mouth for hours. He would reach up to touch his cheeks and find them wet.

If Yirmiyahu had been like the Temple levites, a man of the city rather than a man of the country—if he'd seen God as a masculine and potent deity rather than a bringer of fruits, if he'd seen God as one who protects the People rather than one whom the People protect, if Yirmiyahu had not heard her weeping, if he'd been as a deaf man, if he hadn't been her *navi*, he might have been embittered toward his God. He might have blamed her. He might have shrieked at the irony of Babylon's arrival—as though God had taken action where her People refused to, closing the tomb at Tophet by encamping an army between the hill and the city. If the men and women of Yerusalem wanted to feed the dead now, they would have to offer their own flesh.

But Yirmiyahu could hear God's keening in the Temple, and he knew that her People had abandoned God and not God her People. It was the king's greed, and the complacency of the priests and merchants who advised him, that had kindled the wrath of the great cities in the east. Perhaps God who sobbed now in her Temple had been as alarmed at their coming as anyone in the city. Yirmiyahu didn't know; he only knew that God's lament for her People was violent and overpowering, and it wrenched his heart.

When he rose in the mornings and washed his hands and arms up to the elbows, then his face—in those early mornings of the siege while there was still much water in the city's wells—he comforted himself with the thought that he'd been right to send his wife away, that the anguish in her eyes when he broke covenant with her was atoned for by her distance from their beleaguered city, by her safety in her parents' home in Anathoth in its quiet river valley, days from this starving place, this place of tears.

———

"The granaries are emptied. You know this. There is no food left, and only the dead are eating. Surrender is the only way to preserve the lives in this city." Yirmiyahu pleaded with Zedekiah the king. Long months had passed, and terror had grown in the city. Still Yirmiyahu had beseeched the priests and the guardsmen, had begged outside the doors of the king's house for the gates of the city to be thrown open. The guardsmen had exchanged pale glances at their posts.

Perhaps thinking that so many feet of earth might serve to silence the *navi* where threats seemed not to, the king finally tossed the prophet into a cell beneath his house. There, in the dim light, as weeks passed, Yirmiyahu learned for the first time what *hunger* really was, how there could be a hole in the belly, a hole with teeth around it, threatening to chew up your insides into one great empty place, one that your mind might fall into and never come back.

When the king came to visit his cell one night, it took such effort even to speak, to do anything but groan. "You have known me a long time now, Zedekiah. You know that I do not lie to you, though you don't want to hear me, though you wish to believe I'm mad. Please. There is so little time left." He tugged at his bonds. "Let me free. Let me speak to the people of the city at your side. We can still change what is coming."

"What is coming, what is coming?" Zedekiah began to pace, working himself into a rage. The whites around his eyes showed his fear. "Why do you always bring *these* words, *navi*? You weaken the hearts of my men on the walls. They need to hear words of victory, not your talk of futility and disaster."

"The city will die if you don't yield the gates," Yirmiyahu groaned. "Why won't you understand?" He gazed at the king with sunken, weary eyes. He was a young king, a rash young man—he must have still been a boy not long before. His face was strong with his will, but his eyes were filled always with fear. Fear lived in Zedekiah's skin. Regarding him, Yirmiyahu was certain that whether the king sat or stood, walked or lay down, he must feel the bite of that fear at all times.

With cold dread, Yirmiyahu thought of what was occurring outside the king's house. How the guards now stayed on the city walls, slept and ate there without coming down, or if they did, descending only into the walled, secure courtyard of the king's house. The same courtyard that held a well that was no longer giving water. Outside that walled courtyard, the people of the city locked themselves in their own homes, or went through the streets armed with whatever implements they could find: a shovel, or a tailor's stick, or even the beam from a weaver's loom—Yirmiyahu had seen two men carrying one of those, with a veiled woman following them through the streets, as though they expected to swing the massive beam together and crush the heads of any lurking corpses that stumbled into their path.

"I will not give up this city," Zedekiah shouted. "This is my father's city, and his father's. It is the greatest city in the world. I will not give it up. Beseech your God to protect us!"

"She will not," Yirmiyahu whispered. "You have broken Covenant with her."

The young king hissed. "I have given *monthly* sacrifices at the Temple. The levites fatten on my tithes. Why *shouldn't* God defend us?"

"Sacrifices," Yirmiyahu murmured, sweat stinging his eyes. "She is so weary of sacrifices."

Zedekiah thrust his pale face into Yirmiyahu's. "Listen to me, you fool," he breathed. "Ours is a strong and prosperous city; we have trade routes with every nation of the earth. I *will not* let it fall." Zedekiah's voice shook as he spoke. "Our fathers' fathers lived in tents, Yirmiyahu. In *tents*. Wearing coarse wool and living off milk and gathered roots, like animals. Look at us now, look at all our fathers built. In my palace there are purple fabrics from Tyre and Sidon, ointments from Kemet. We have markets, scribes, educated men who chatter in the evening at our gates. We have strong men on the walls and strong gods to protect us. I have no intention of surrendering this city. I have three sons and I will leave this city to them intact. With its walls standing. And you, *navi* or no, you are going to rot in this cell where your words can make no man's heart quail, until Babylon marches home."

Yirmiyahu was silent a moment, weariness heavy on his shoulders. "Purple fabrics," he murmured. "Men who talk at the gates. The Pharaoh of Kemet said such things as these to our Lawgiver, about the cities of Kemet. Yet Kemet was not given the Covenant and the Law. We were. No nation, though it have decorated tombs taller than mountains and all the world's perfumes—no nation can be called great if some of its people starve, or are sold to beds in other cities, or are forgotten, or sacrificed to the dead to make a few men feel safe."

And then words, God's words, filled Yirmiyahu's ears and his chest, as though God had heard the king and was crying out her reply, until her *navi* gave in and murmured her words aloud:

> What use to me are perfumes from Sheba,
> or sweet cane from far countries?
> Your burnt offerings are not acceptable,
> Your sacrifices do not please me.

He caught the king's eyes with his. Zedekiah's eyes were pale with restrained fear, Yirmiyahu's were bloodshot, exhausted. "God is leaving the city," the *navi* groaned. "She cannot stay—the Covenant is shattered; God's ears are violated with the screams of her People."

He closed his eyes, leaned back against the wall, as a vision—a terrible witnessing of the future—poured into his mind with the words. "This is no great city, O king. And I—I have seen—I have seen with my eyes—how your resistance will end. God sees what will happen; it is before her eyes day and night. So many deaths. So many. And as many nights as the gates are closed against Babylon, closing all of us inside, those many nights the dead gather in your streets. You must—*must*—lie down, let the king of Babylon place his boot on your neck. Otherwise, what is left of the city when he takes it will be burned with fire, its walls broken like the walls of Yeriho, our People felled like an oak or a terebinth, leaving only a stump behind." He opened his eyes, saw Zedekiah's horrified face, the king's hand making the sign against evil. "Your wife will be put to death after the soldiers of that foreign land touch her. Your sons, Zedekiah, your three sons will be killed as you watch, knives to their bellies. And the king of Babylon will cut out your eyes, wanting your sons' deaths to be the last sight you remember in your long life as a captive."

"*Be silent!*"

Yirmiyahu laughed bitterly and felt the laughter would break him apart. "Do you think I haven't tried to be? I am silent and my bones groan within me, I cannot sleep all the night for the roaring of the words rushing through me. I cannot be silent."

———

Though his eyes were open in the shadow at the bottom of the well, Yirmiyahu lay in an exhaustion that resembled sleep, his body shivering in his improvised coat of defiled and tattered cloth. His mind moved, slow as kelp in the Middle Sea to the west, into other dreams of the past.

For Yirmiyahu, that year of the siege had been a bitter struggle, one fought over men's hearts and with no weapons keener than words. When he was not in a cell, he spent the year at Baruch's shop. The sunlight through Baruch's boarded windows had been a blessing, as had been the silent way Baruch cared for him and took down the prophecies and warnings he spoke. In Yirmiyahu's memory, clear as a lake bed seen through unrippled water, Baruch the scribe sat behind his desk with a papyrus scroll spread before him. Baruch: his name meant "blessed," and he was: a man who could afford bread and who knew how to read and write Hebrew letters with a speed and facility Yirmiyahu himself lacked. Baruch was bald, so that the sunlight shone on his head as on a warrior's shield. His little shop sat against the northern wall and the light came through a window on the south, at the shop's front. Baruch slept in a little room upstairs, and Yirmiyahu slept on a few blankets before the desk, ever since he'd sent his wife away and sold his small house.

Often in the hour before the sun dropped beneath the south wall and cast them into night, Yirmiyahu would pace across the shop—four strides each way—and pour words from his mouth like water from a ewer. When God sent the words like a river, the *navi* could not dam or channel it; it rushed through him. At times he nearly shattered apart with the force of the emotions sweeping through him.

> A voice is heard in Rama
> cries and bitter weeping
> God is weeping for her children
> she refuses to be comforted
> for they are gone

Baruch's hand moved with speed and certainty, sketching with his stylus the angular shapes that were letters, the gift God had given to the Lawgiver many generations before, that her words might be heard whenever the Lawgiver's scroll was read.

But God hadn't stopped speaking, and Yirmiyahu wept as her words, terrible words, rushed through him. Ever since the gates closed, those words had been words of horror and dismay, words of warning and of pleading, words telling of the destruction that was already creeping within the city. Sometimes the recitation would end long before the sun fell, for Yirmiyahu would collapse in grief and lie on the floor, fighting for breath. Then Baruch would quietly set aside his stylus, stopper the flask of blueberry ink, and breathe slowly over the scroll to dry it. After a while he would roll up the scroll and bind it with a yellow string, then kneel beside Yirmiyahu and sit with him, not speaking, with his head bent in prayer. Sometimes, Baruch just watched his friend's face. Baruch sat with him through the long watches, listening to the occasional scream in the streets. He would sigh and settle his legs more comfortably, set his hand on the *navi*'s shoulder, and wait for his grief to pass.

Some days the words came early, and Yirmiyahu would lie for long hours in a stupor on his pallet below the window, as the words of God shook him, the cries of God for her People, for her spouse who'd forsaken her, cries that tore through Yirmiyahu's body like shrieks as he lay there. On those days, as Yirmiyahu lay twitching on the pallet, Baruch paid an assistant to take the scroll on which he'd recorded Yirmiyahu's words and read them aloud at the Temple steps or at the gates, foretelling death to the city and pleading for the gates to open and the people to be fed— even if this meant they were fed bread and meat out of the hands of Babylonian soldiers. Baruch even paid for a guard to protect the assistant, in case the priests' anger should turn violent as the words were read. Baruch did this to honor Yirmiyahu, the *navi*, who'd told him on the first day he entered his shop of his private covenant with God, a covenant he'd made the day the gates shut. His promise to her to speak to the priests at the Temple steps and to the guards at the wall each day without fail before the sun reached its noon.

One evening Yirmiyahu opened his eyes and saw the day's last faint light through the cracks in the wood barring the shop's window. Baruch was sitting by him, but Yirmiyahu ignored the scribe, gazed at the cracks of sunlight in the window—for a little while he did not recognize it as the shop's window, and for some reason the lines of sunlight terrified him. He whispered:

> How lonely is the city that was full of people,
> How like a widow.
> She weeps bitterly in the night,
> with tears on her cheeks;
> she has none to comfort her.

Gazing at the broken pieces of light, he saw the dead gnawing on crippled children in the shadow of the broken wall. He saw soldiers marching through the ashen ruins of the city's houses, their conical helmets and their spears with shining bronze heads, and they were not soldiers of the People.

A sharp slap across his cheek. He turned and blinked, saw Baruch there. Slowly he felt the floor under his body, cool under his head. Baruch was frowning. His lips moved, and Yirmiyahu focused and heard the scribe's words: "Enough, friend. Where is your hope? Where is your conviction that the words a *navi* brings can change hearts? That the city can be restored? Where is your hope, huh?"

Yirmiyahu's lips felt very dry, his eyes also. A soreness in his muscles. "I am thirsty," he whispered.

Then Baruch grinned and grasped his friend's arms, pulling him up from the floor.

"Why do you fight the priesthood so?" Baruch demanded after he'd filled a clay bowl with water and held it to Yirmiyahu's lips for a while. The priests had begun threatening Baruch for harboring one they'd cast from their number, but Baruch was known and honored by the merchants and professed to fear the priests little. In any case, a few of the younger levites, a very few, had begun coming in secret to his shop during the evening dark to listen, and to ask questions of "the mad *navi*."

Now the scribe gently set the emptied bowl aside, and Yirmiyahu leaned against Baruch's desk a moment, recovering his breath. "Until there is justice in the city," he rasped, "we are as a dry well that waters no growth. We are as parched earth, from which even God's skillful hands can grow only withered and sickly things."

"They're going to kill you, you know." Baruch's voice was very quiet. "Someday soon."

Yirmiyahu reached with trembling fingers and tapped the scroll with his fingertips. "They cannot kill these. They cannot kill or silence the words of God." He caught Baruch's eyes. "And it is these, and not I, that will nourish our starving people and open the gates of the city before everything is lost."

"Huh," Baruch grunted, and bent back to the work. "I fear you are wrong, friend," the scribe muttered after a moment, his hand moving swiftly across the dry papyrus. "The scrolls are fragile, too. A mere splash of water and they crumble apart. They are more mortal than men."

───

Hoshekh filled the well as wine fills a cup.

Yirmiyahu's skin was burning a little. He slept fitfully and woke finally with sweat cold on his face and back. A fever had broken. He breathed shallowly for a while, watching the stars, praying. Then slipped back into a half sleep.

"Fear is a sickness." He could hear her, hear Miriam's voice. He slipped, eager as a fish into water, a fish released from a hand over the side of a boat, into a dream of that night, their last night together. She had dampened his brow with a cloth and then cleaned his wounds; it was the day he had spoken against Tophet, before the siege, the day the levites at the Temple had pelted him with rocks, pursuing him through the street before he'd been able to get through to the door of his house. And when he'd reached the house at last, they had almost torn down the door before leaving. At least they *had* left.

Miriam's hands on his face and limbs were soothing, calming. "Fear is a very great sickness. It makes them weak, husband. It's like a fever. They toss in their beds with it. They'll give anything up, or hurt anyone, to feel safe again." She whispered, "This might hurt, husband," and touched the cloth to a gash in Yirmiyahu's leg. He hissed and stiffened as she cleaned grit out of the tear in his skin. His leg all about that gash was bruised and swollen, but the rock had not broken it. By some miracle, nothing had broken.

"They're like the gleaner in Anathoth," Miriam said softly as she dabbed the wound. "Hannah. Do you remember her?"

Yirmiyahu forced himself to breathe deeply, easily. "The girl with the dreams?"

"Yes, the girl with the dreams." Miriam sighed. "She was afraid, too."

The girl Hannah had been one of the poorest in that little farming village; her father and brother had died in a fever. They had not risen from the ground afterward; it had been an ordinary fever. But it had left Hannah without resources. In Anathoth, Yirmiyahu recalled bitterly, the Law was still followed, the Covenant still kept. As required by the Covenant with the God who nourishes, the reapers of the fields left any grain that fell and did not stoop to pick it up; they left it for any who needed it. Joining other women who were without husbands or fathers, Hannah walked the fields each harvest, following the reapers, gathering up the grain that fell, taking it back to her tiny house to feed herself during the cold months.

Thinking of those fields, Yirmiyahu was taken suddenly by a fierce longing for Anathoth, for a quieter life studying the Law and preparing for the priesthood, back before he had ever heard any voice calling him in the night. Before he had lived in this sweltering, populous city, where the streets were noisy and most people did not hear God.

The village of Anathoth had pitied Hannah, yet most people tried not to think about her—not because she was poor, but because of what she did about her dreams. At first, night after night, terrors took her in her sleep and made her scream within her little house. The village's wise woman brought herbs and tried to calm her sleep, but the herbs didn't work very well. "She is too sick with her fear, I cannot cure it," the woman confessed to the town's elders, her eyes moist with tears.

In time Hannah found her own way of coping with her dreams. She began taking the town's young men into her house by night; they would come to her at first in the fields at harvest as she carried grain back home, and out of sight of the reapers they would walk with her. Then they began slipping furtively into her house by night, or on hot afternoons while most of the town slept. Hannah was very quiet, and though some of the town's women stared hard at her closed door, they heard no moans or cries within. Yet they stopped talking with her—even the other gleaners did, and Hannah would walk a little behind the others at harvest, gathering what she might, a lonely ghost of the past, hungry and silent.

One evening, shortly after he married Miriam but before they began packing for the move to Yerusalem, Yirmiyahu came home from talking with the elders about all the things he must remember when he came before the priests in Yerusalem and asked to be one of them. Yirmiyahu came in through the door into the little rooms of his house humming, and then stopped, startled. There were Miriam and Hannah, sitting together by the cookpot, making dinner. Miriam glanced over her shoulder at him and her smile caught at his heart. "I asked Hannah to eat with us, husband," she said. "I hope you aren't displeased?"

Another man in Anathoth might have raged at not having been asked first. But Yirmiyahu was newly married and drunk as with wine on Miriam's kisses and her laughter and her voice. So he simply sat across the cookpot from them, looking bewildered. Miriam finished their stew, then instructed Hannah on where to find a half loaf of bread in one of the baskets at the room's corner. As they ate, Miriam talked, sharing stories of her childhood or asking Yirmiyahu's opinions on matters of discussion in the town; she listened to his replies attentively with soft, laughing eyes. Though Hannah was mostly silent, she smiled warmly when Miriam broke off a piece of bread and gave it to her, and once she reached out and gripped Miriam's hand so tightly that Miriam winced.

"Why did we have a guest?" Yirmiyahu asked his wife later that night, holding her in his arms in their bed, panting softly after their love.

Miriam gazed at him, looking very serious, though her face was still flushed, strands of her hair sweaty across her face. "She has no one to hear her, husband. It hurt to see how lonely she was."

"Hear her? She was very quiet—I don't remember her saying much."

"Yes, she did," Miriam said, and Yirmiyahu remembered the smiles and the grip on Miriam's hand. He had often seen women communicating across a street with a look or a turn of their shoulder. Perhaps women had a language that didn't need words.

"Miriam, I am not sure," Yirmiyahu murmured, "that she is a good woman to have in my house."

"Because she invites men," Miriam said quietly, her tone still very serious. "But no one has tried to stone her for it, and no one has made her leave. And the women of Anathoth ignore it and get their husbands to ignore it, as long as she doesn't invite a man who is married." Miriam's eyes were soft in the dark. "We all heard her screams, husband. Something happened to her as a child. Something her father did to her. She's very afraid to sleep without someone else near her or holding her."

———

As Miriam tended him with the cloth and with her soft hands, Yirmiyahu tried again to understand what his wife was telling him. Always she seemed to have something worth listening to, but it was not always easy to understand what she meant. He thought of the white-robed men chasing him through the streets with their rocks, their round, furious, terrified eyes. He thought of the way Hannah's eyes had often been round like that, showing their whites.

"The gleaner," Yirmiyahu murmured. "I need to pity the men at the Temple steps. That's what you're saying."

"I'm saying they're afraid and ill, husband," Miriam said quietly. "I don't pity them. They hurt you." Her voice caught, and Yirmiyahu closed his hand around her fingers for a moment. His eyes searched Miriam's face and saw something he'd missed before, in the year since they'd settled into this little house. A little wrinkling around her eyes, and a softness in them. Yirmiyahu felt a pang of regret. In taking her to this city, he had removed her from all the women she knew. His wife was lonely here. And when she had suffered a terrible loss earlier that year, the most terrible of losses, she had shut herself within this little house, and no women had come to see her. Her husband had stayed home more of the time for a while, and had held her in his arms, but had been at a loss as to how to comfort her. Those lines around her eyes—were those loss or were they loneliness, with no one to hear her?

"I am sorry," he whispered. "Sorry we are here."

He tried to lift himself, groaning at the pain of his bruises. Her gentle hand on his chest pressed him down. Her eyes deep with worry in the light of the tiny oil lamp on the table. His vision had gone blurry for a moment. He saw in his mind, so clearly, the shambling dead beneath the altar at Tophet. He hadn't told Miriam of it; he didn't know if he could speak of it to her yet without weeping.

Miriam's lips brushed his cheek. "Lie still, my husband." He heard the plop of the cloth in the ewer, then the drip of water as she lifted it. His vision cleared, and he saw her lift the cloth to his face. It was cool and moist against his cheek. As she looked down at his eyes, a smile awoke in hers, and he warmed to see it. "I've changed my mind. On your belly, my husband."

He rolled over with a groan and a violent ache of his muscles. She helped him, then took her hands away, and when they came back and settled on his shoulders, they were moist with oil. Her hands moved over the muscles of his shoulders and back, rubbing in an ointment that flickered with heat along his skin, then cooled after her hands passed, making him gasp. "Where did you get that?"

"From the widow who keeps her booth by the Sheep Gate." She spoke softly, her lips not far from his ear. "I overpaid her. She looks so thin."

"It's wonderful, my wife." He started to breathe more deeply, the pain in his back dulling, though the aches in his arms—where stones had struck him as he shielded his head—still burned. But then Miriam brought more oil and gently ran her hands up his arms, and her lips placed slow kisses on his back. He shivered. "That feels even better," he murmured.

"And this?" she whispered, catching his earlobe gently in her lips, her breath moist and soft.

Before long he found himself on his back again, holding her in his arms, ignoring the aches that remained. The night had turned suddenly gentle and soft in their home, and he parted her garments, whispering to her from the People's most ancient song of love, a song of laughter and tears, a song of the sweetness of a man's union with a woman and a God's union with a People who had captured her heart: "Oh my beloved, you are to me as the lily among the thorns."

"As the apple tree among the trees of the wood," she whispered back, "is my love among the sons." She kissed him lightly, and when she drew away her eyes were heated. "And his fruit is sweet to my taste." She laughed, clear as a bell, and touched him. "Make haste, my love, make haste, and be like a gazelle or a young stag on the mountains of spices."

And he moved within her, slowly, for he was still terribly sore.

He woke now, still caught in the joy of it, the touch of her skin on his, the way she held him tightly, warmly inside her. And as he drew in a shuddering breath, his eyes open but unseeing, he was suddenly back in the stench of the dead and the aloneness of his cistern tomb. The darkness around him, so different from that gentle night, was as a stab in the belly. He yearned for her. He yearned now for fresh water and sunlight on his skin and for every sweet thing he had ever known, but especially for her.

SECOND DAY: IF ALL GOD'S PEOPLE WERE PROPHETS

L AUGHTER FAR overhead; living men stood up there, staring down into the well. Yirmiyahu looked up at them, their silhouettes against the circle of sunlight. "Let me out!" he began to beg, his rasping voice echoing in the cold throat of the well.

More laughter and muffled talk. Another bundle shoved over the brink of the well, smaller than the last. He tensed as it dropped.

This one had a gaping wound in its side and its wrists were bound. The fall broke its legs and split open its belly. Still it struggled to get on its knees in the dim light, its intestines spilling from its abdomen in a rush of guts and viscous fluid. Its eyes were wide, its jaws snapping as it toppled over and rolled toward him in the mud.

For a few breaths, as the broken creature moaned and wallowed, Yirmiyahu just leaned against the stones of the wall, watching it. His body felt heavy and cold. I have turned to stone, he thought, I am part of the wall.

This creature had been a girl, perhaps twelve winters old. Maybe less. Yirmiyahu stumbled to his feet on weak and aching legs as it snapped its jaws and fought to get close to him.

For a long moment he hesitated, stunned.

It had been a girl, a little girl.

The creature's milky eyes were fixed on him; its mouth opened in a long growl. His heart hammered in his chest.

"I'm sorry," the prophet whispered, "I'm so sorry."

Stepping forward, he took its head in his hands, holding it tightly at arm's length—the creature was very strong—and dragged the corpse to the wall. He slammed the head into the wall, hearing a crack of bone. The creature kept writhing and kicking, trying to twist its head in his hands to bite him; he slammed it into the stones again and again. He kept hitting the creature's head into the wall until it was still at last. Then he stood over it numbly, gazing down at that shattered body, the likeness of God violated and defaced. His hands hung limply at his sides, defiled and unclean. He moaned, a sound not unlike the moan of the dead but voicing anguish and horror that the dead could never know, the dead who were incapable of regret or shame.

He gazed down, saw bits of flesh in the mud and on his clothes but no blood. No blood. The girl's chest had torn further open; a few ribs now jabbed out through the skin and the torn garment it wore. Yirmiyahu gazed up at the circle of night over his head. They would drop other dead in after him; there might be another, and another after that. If he was to survive, he would need more than clothing; he would need some weapon or tool with which to put an end to these unclean corpses that hungered and did not lie still. He cried out the name of his God, begging her forgiveness for the violation he intended to commit.

Sweating, he reached down and took hold of one of the dead girl's ribs and pulled it free, breaking a length of it, snapping it away from the rib cage. He held the rib before him like a long, white knife. The body below sank slowly into the mud. Yirmiyahu wished he might murmur the Words of Going, but his throat closed and he couldn't get them out. What right had he to wish her rest after violating her body, and when none of his deeds and none of his words had sufficed to protect her, or any of the city's children, from this end?

"Death has come up into our windows," Yirmiyahu whispered as he held the gleaming rib in his hand. He gazed at its jagged end and everything it portended: the wrecking of the bodies of children and women, and in them the very body of God, kicked aside and left shaking in the street by the levites and the merchants and all who ignored the hungering of famished bodies outside their houses or the bleeding of raped bodies in the alleys behind. And he thought of the defiled bodies of the dead lurching between sleeping houses, some with ribs like this one exposed amid torn and gaping flesh, glinting in the light of the moon and the stars.

How the impoverished men and women in the city had hastened to find wood to bar the one window in their home. In the early nights of the siege, when the plague was really just beginning, the windows had been open to the night air, and in the quiet hours, dark shapes had appeared in the windows, a glint of eyes in the starlight, hands clutching the sills. They had crawled through, reaching for the warm life within. Grabbing the leg or the arm of whoever slept inside the house and pulling that flesh to their waiting mouths. Men and women would wake to the shock of teeth cutting into their bodies. They would wrestle with their attackers in the dark, but it was too late. Some would be devoured while they writhed and cried out; those in the next house would cover their ears and pretend they heard nothing. Others lay feverish with terrible wounds once the dead were sated and wandered out, until they fell into a sleep without breathing and then woke with a hunger as intense as that of a dry well for rain.

Yirmiyahu ran his fingertip across the broken, jagged edge of the rib, feeling the sharpness without cutting his skin. For a moment, even in his horror, he marveled at it. He held it up, gazing at the long, graceful curve of the bone. The first woman had been made from one of these. It was a marvel. He remembered suddenly how, in the early part of the siege, he had knocked on the door of the widow's shop near the Sheep Gate in the hot morning—for no reason other than that she had been a friend of his wife's. He'd heard someone moving inside the booth, but no answer came to his call. Then a thump, like a body fallen. Uneasily, he forced the door and slipped into the dark booth. Something moved near him, then he saw her silhouette and knew by its movement that it was not her. He leapt backward through the door, into the sunlight, and it followed him out. It was terrible. It had the widow's face, except that the nose had been chewed away, and one eye was gone. One arm hung broken at its side; the other reached for him.

That a body made to bear life into the world could be turned into *that*.

———

Each time he woke, dozens of times, clutching the rib, the world was still dark. And so cold. A levite, Yirmiyahu had always had a roof over his head—even if this past year it had only been the roof of Baruch's shop—and a rug to wrap himself in. He hadn't understood the cold before, the way your hands could clench up and stop working, the way your body shook as though coming apart. He breathed through his teeth, for his nose burned. He tried to remember the sun, the day heat that beat on his arms. Thought of the day, months before, when he'd led the children to break the granaries behind the Temple. Their bodies had run with sweat; by the time they reached the tall, tomb-like shapes of the grain silos, each of the children (and he himself) had been covered in a layer of brown dust that stuck to them. Children made of earth.

Yirmiyahu had leaped up the sod ramp to the first silo, stripped away his shirt, taken up a great shovel, and broken apart the locks. A heave of his arms and the door to the silo shot open. Grain came running out, a rush of golden beads. Priests tried to stop them, rushing at them from the courtyard, and there was a bitter fight behind the Temple grounds, a more brutal fight than Yirmiyahu had ever imagined. The children kicked and bit at the priests who grabbed them, and gouged at their eyes with reaching fingers; Yirmiyahu saw a white-robed priest knock down a small boy with a blow to the head. With a scream, Yirmiyahu threw himself bodily into the priest and bore him to the ground, clouting the man's head with his fists. There were the high shrieks of children, the curses of grown men, and the thickening cloud of dust that so many wrestling feet kicked up into the air. In that haze, an anger took Yirmiyahu that burned hotter than any he'd ever known. He lifted the shovel in both hands and swung it, slamming its blunt blade into men's bodies. His chest was soon damp with spatters of blood. He could hardly see anything; he just swung whenever he came upon a man-sized shape, screaming words in Hebrew and other loud cries that were not words. "Elohim adonai!" he howled, "Elohi, Elohi, my God, my God!"

At last they routed the priests. The children who could filled the bowls and jars they'd brought with grain, then ran away into the streets, disappearing. Yirmiyahu leaned a moment on his shovel, fighting to breathe against the tightness in his chest. Then he staggered to where one of the girls lay moaning in the dust, her head bleeding. He tore strips from his clothes and tried to bind wounds; the dust settled slowly, the shapes of grain silos and Temple walls and bodies gradually becoming more distinct and real in the haze around him. One child died in his arms, choking on blood, trying to speak and unable to make any sounds but that horrible sucking sound of blood going into the lungs. Then the child in Yirmiyahu's arms shuddered and was still, and later the king's guards found the *navi* like that, holding that broken body.

They took Yirmiyahu, bound his wrists to a pole in the courtyard of the king's house, and beat him. He cursed them each time a fist or a foot struck his ribs, and the blows kept coming until he hung from his wrists, something broken. He hung there and rasped. Blood dripped from his lower lip, sweat from his brow and hair. And gradually, amid the roar of his body and the desperate wheezing of his breath, he realized someone was talking to him and had been for a while. He turned his head, clenching his teeth against the pain. One eye was too swollen, but through the other he saw a thin man with a pale face and many rings on his fingers. His clothes were finely made and rich in hue, something maybe from the Sea People. His beard, which had the newness of a first-growth beard, was trimmed carefully and braided; his green eyes watched the prophet warily.

"Zedekiah," Yirmiyahu breathed. He had never seen this man before, this man barely more than a youth. But he was certain who the man was.

The king stopped what he'd been saying and smiled faintly. "So you *are* listening to me," he said.

Yirmiyahu just looked at him. A rage burned just beneath his skin, but it took too much effort even to breathe. He hung there and kept his eye on the young king.

"If it's grain you want," the king said quietly, "you can buy it."

Yirmiyahu laughed shortly, then fought for breath to speak. "Half those children—are—orphans. The other half—bond slaves. The city's children—suffer—for your pride. You revoked— the *yovel*—the year—of God's—favor." It took so much out of him, the effort of speech, and the last word fell into a sharp groan.

The king crouched, like a boy looking into a pool, and his face was only a breath from Yirmiyahu's. His eyes were intent, but Yirmiyahu could see the fear in them. "Babylon crouches on the Mount of Olives watching us, like an old crow. Like a *flock* of old crows—all those bowmen with their feathered shafts. This is no time for the *yovel*," he hissed. "I will not destroy you—you are a holy man, *navi*. But why do you stir up the people of the street?"

Yirmiyahu began to laugh slowly, then his body shook with it. Zedekiah leaned back on his heels, his face aghast; the prophet laughed, his mouth open, his body heaving painfully where he hung. Yirmiyahu felt moisture on his cheeks, knew that he was crying. He stopped laughing, panted for breath. He gasped out the words of God that poured through him in a sudden wild rush:

> The snorting of their horses has been heard in Dan,
> at the neighing of their stallions all the land shakes.
> They come, they devour the land and all that fills it,
> The city, and all who dwell in it.
> My joy is gone, my grief gnaws at me,
> My heart is sick within me.
> Listen, the cry of the daughter of my People
> Fills the north and the south of my land.
> On your garments I see the blood of your sons and your daughters.
> Now listen.
> Now look, Zedekiah.

> The dead will fill your city, and the sky filled with crows,
> None can scare them away.
> And they will silence in the cities of Yudah and in the streets
> of Yerusalem
> the voice of mirth and the voice of gladness,
> the voice of the bridegroom and the voice of the bride,
> for this land will become a desert.

As the last words fell from Yirmiyahu's lips, he lowered his head, looking only at the bruises on his legs and the hard pebbles and dirt of the courtyard of the king's house. He was empty now, and he felt a breeze pass over his skin and then through him, as though there were holes in his body. He just breathed.

"You're mad," Zedekiah whispered.

The prophet made no answer. After a while there was the rustle of the young king's clothes and his steps passing quickly away across the courtyard. The rustle of fine linens brushed back from where they hung across a door. Then nothing. Yirmiyahu was aware of the sounds, but he gave them little thought. He lifted his head wearily and felt the sun on his face. His wrists ached where they were bound, but that hardly mattered to him, for all of him was an ache except for the cool empty space inside him where the words had passed through and then gone. From his one eye he watched the wide and uninhabited sky. Somewhere he heard the howl of a jackal. When the king's men came to untie his wrists and set him free in the city, they found him sleeping.

———

Yirmiyahu found a new reserve of strength when the hole in his sky lightened again. He climbed unsteadily to his feet, his hands grasping the stones of the cistern wall; then, with slow steps, he began to circle the well, always with his hands on the wall before him. It was calming, these slow circles, his legs wading through the wet mud. He felt very warm and did not know why. Lifting his fingers to his lips, he found them hot to the touch. Thirst made a desert of his throat until it hurt to breathe. Still he walked in his circles, each one tracing the edges of his world. The stench in the well was terrible, and his eyes watered. At one point he stopped and gazed up at the faraway circle in his sky and screamed for help or mercy. He called out many times. He called Zedekiah's name, and the name of one of his guards that he remembered, and Baruch's name, and Miriam's. Many times. His throat ached. He could not tell how loud he was calling; his voice sounded distant to him, detached from his own lips and throat.

He realized that he'd fallen silent for some time, and that the mud was sucking hungrily at his thighs as he forced his way through it in his slow circles. Without halting his steps, he closed his eyes. He kept walking. Kept walking.

———

On an evening very early in the siege, Yirmiyahu had burst into Baruch's shop, his hair flying wildly about his face. The Sabbath was coming. "Quickly!" he called to Baruch, who was sitting at his scribe's desk. "Before the sun sets—write down these words. These words, my friend!"

> The days are coming when I will make a new Covenant with my People, who have broken our old one. They will hear my Law in their hearts, and I will be their God, and they will be my People. There will be no need of priest or teacher or for one to say to his brother, Know these ways of our God, for they will all know me, from the smallest child to the richest man. I will forgive them, and clasp them to me, and nourish them, and no longer remember their darkness.

"A fantasy," Baruch told him later as he shut and barred the shop's one window. "The world will always be inhabited by the eaters and the eaten. It is how things are."

"But it breaks her heart." Yirmiyahu had washed his face and elbows ritually, preparing for the day's last meal—a meager one it would be, a bowl of grains. Baruch sat and made his stylus dance across the papyrus, writing down the words Yirmiyahu had brought. Yirmiyahu glanced at him, at the speed and evenness with which his hands moved, a speed he could never match. Something full welled up inside him. The words the *navi* brought *would* save the city—they had to—and there would be so much work to do to mend the torn Covenant and make the city once again a place to which God might be welcomed, the way a man might welcome his bride to a peaceful and wholesome house, swept clean. With bowls of stew and loaves of bread readied for passing around a wide circle of kin seated on their banquet cushions. A place to feast together, a place where God might laugh with her People, even as a bride and her husband might laugh together in a good house and eat with their family before her husband swept her into his arms and carried her to bed for a night soft with their loving.

There was so much to be done. The city *would* be saved. Surely the city would be saved. Did not God's words about a new Covenant promise it? Yirmiyahu clung to that, and his blood thrilled within him, demanding action. The mending must begin now, this evening—it couldn't wait for the accord of priests or king.

"Baruch! You must call the children into the shop, the children in those streets, who are without fathers. Teach them to write as you do. Then they will not be hungry."

Baruch looked up, startled. "Who is to pay for it?"

"No one." Yirmiyahu smiled, this sudden hope within him as heady as spiced wine. "But you have an hour after dark, between when we eat and when we sleep—we spend it now in idle talk, or sometimes I just sit silently recovering from the words of God while you write. But this is more important than talking, more important even than the scroll."

"More important than the words of God?"

Yirmiyahu dried his hands on a ragged cloth and spoke with passion: "Obeying the words of God is always more important than talking about them."

"Huh," Baruch grunted. "Huh." His brow wrinkled in thought, his eyes glinting. "If you bring those orphans, Yirmiyahu, and if I do not need to feed them, and if they do not shit on my floor, then in the hour before bed, I will teach them the aleph-bet."

"You are a warrior for God, my friend." Yirmiyahu clasped Baruch's arm, grinning. But Baruch pushed him away hastily: "Your hair is dripping on my scrolls!"

Yirmiyahu stepped back, grinning. "Where you see a child who may shit on your floor, I see a child who will one day be a great scribe, or a man of business, or a secretary to the king."

"Huh."

"And one day you will see the man that child became, and I will hear you laugh."

Then they prayed and sang in hoarse voices a welcome to the Sabbath. And when the Sabbath was past, Yirmiyahu ran from the shop and went to gather up children. And of course Baruch *did* give the children grain to eat and water to drink, as he taught them those stark Hebrew letters that had been designed centuries ago to be chiseled into tablets of rock and not scrawled into scrolls of papyrus. Baruch could not look at their thin bodies and then hold back his grain. But often after that, he and Yirmiyahu were hungrier.

Sometimes Baruch told the children stories afterward, tales he had heard or read, tales of heroes, of David and his Mighty Men when they lived in the Cave in the wilderness. Of Benaiah, who on a day of snow leaped into a narrow canyon and fought one of the dead with his bare hands, tearing its head from its shoulders. And Eleazar the Ahohite, who stood with David, just the two of them, in a field of barley, with the dead in a circle closing round them. Eleazar and David fought long into the dusk, their spearheads flashing in the dim light, while the dead pressed in on them, hands clutching at them, mouths open in long moans. But as the moon rose, both warriors walked away victorious through a field of motionless dead.

And there was the time that David had been encamped in the hills near Bet Lechem, when the town had been infested with the wakeful dead. Looking down at the little houses and the shambling figures in the streets, David laughed. "Oh, if someone would only bring me water to drink from the well of Bet Lechem by that gate!" And three of his men heard and fought their way into the town, felling the dead with their spears. Two of them held off the dead while a third pulled up a bucket from the well. Then they ran back into the hills, the bronze heads of their spears dripping with gore. When they brought David the water, his face went very still, in shock at what they had tried, what they had done. He rose and took the bucket in his hands. He would not drink from it, but poured it out in a libation to God. "Far be it from me before God that I should drink the blood of my men," he said. "At the risk of their lives they brought me this water."

The children sat on the floor and gazed up at Baruch with hungry eyes as they devoured his stories of their People, that nourishment they needed as desperately as they needed grain. Yirmiyahu, too. He felt like a child again, listening to the wild stories of their ancestors. Some evenings Yirmiyahu wondered if Baruch, too, was a kind of *navi*, and if the fruit of God might come to the People through the scribe's tales, as much as through Yirmiyahu's messages. He would have to ask Baruch to write some of these stories on the scroll.

Those evenings spent in the People's remembrances of David and Benaiah and Eleazar were the only moments of peace and wholeness in Yirmiyahu's life since Miriam had gone. At these moments he felt something like happiness again.

Yet there would still be mornings when he woke shuddering from dreams filled with God's quiet sobs, and as he lay breathing, he'd find himself whispering Miriam's name, his face wet with tears.

He had sent her away. It was something he didn't want to think about, but the memory of the pain in her eyes came to him when he wasn't wary, in the moments before sleep or after waking, or worse—in the quiet hours between, when his dreaming self would walk through a wood of cedars, tall and dark, some forest of Lebanon in the north, a wild place. All through those trees he would hear her weeping, a sound that tore at him until he was frantic, his hair flying about his face as he leaped through the trees and underbrush but could never find her. A few times he thought he caught a glimpse of her from behind, a figure with long, unveiled hair and a dress the color of the sand; he would run for her, calling out, then awake before he reached her, his eyes opening at the very moment she turned to face him.

Now, in the well, where there were no mouths to feed, no kings to battle, no holy work that kept grief at bay, that memory found him and fastened to him like a great leech in the mud, and he lay against the wall as it drank from him.

As dawn slipped into his house with the sound of voices in the street on that last day, Yirmiyahu had lain beside his wife in their bed, his body sore and stiff, the wounds on his legs aching from the previous day's stoning, though much relieved by Miriam's ointment. The *navi* had watched her sleeping, her soft body, her graceful eyelids, the delicate curve of her jaw. He thought how beautifully she was made, how God, who had birthed her into the world, must have meant for the whole world to look like that, like her. At peace, glowing with beauty. Yirmiyahu smelled her hair and caressed the long strands of it. The *navi*'s task, he thought, in bringing God's words to the People, was to call the People to be worthy of God, and worthy of such a woman as his wife, made in God's likeness.

The first time he'd seen her, she was dancing in the barley during the Feast of Tents, with all about her the pavilions and booths of the People, and above her a night filled with stars. He had danced with her, and asked her name and her mother's, and she had laughed when he told her he was a levite by birth, like her, for she did not believe him. After they danced they had kissed, and the touch of her lips on his left him dizzy, and when he stumbled back to his father's tent he'd realized how sharp, how bright in color were the tents and the people and the wild thyme growing by the path.

The wedding bowl had cracked beneath their feet. He remembered how she had hummed as she moved about their first home in Anathoth, and the way she cried softly a few months later as she packed his levite's robes and her green linen gown—a gift of her mother's—for the long walk into the hills to Yerushalem. The words they'd spoken together when he came into the room to hold her. The soft warmth of her beside him as they finished the packing together.

They had gone in the summer, and on the first night of their journey, as they laid out their bedding beneath a stand of terebinths, the cicadas in the branches made a roar with their wings, a droning that drowned out all the world's other sounds, wrapping husband and wife in a hum of privacy, the two of them alone together in the summer night. He remembered the gentleness of her kisses on his throat, the soft noises they had made together, the way she lay in his arms afterward and dreamed with him of children.

But they had also lost a child in this house, in this bed. That time Miriam had wakened in the chill hour before dawn to a flow of blood from her thighs, and her scream had awakened him. He'd held her, too numb for words, too shattered by the sight to rise and light the lamp; they wept together in the darkness of their small house. Everything in him had felt crushed and beaten by the sight of that blood. In this city the very bodies of women were violated and defiled in the narrow streets beneath the wall's shadow; their very God was violated in the rape and desecration of those who bore her likeness. The city was desecrated, unable any longer to bear or sustain life, and the uncleanness and disease of the People had become so great that no house in Yerusalem could now be safe from its touch—even his own house, even his own bed.

At last he rose stiffly, gathered up the defiled sheets, and comforted his wife, though his breast felt hollow and empty as a dry well.

Things had been different after that. There had been a fierceness to her kisses, and a sorrow that welled up in both of them at times, so that they sat quietly by the cookpot some evenings without speaking. Some *hoshekh* had crept into their house.

And Miriam hadn't conceived again, though she asked often for her husband's touch and sometimes wept afterward; he, for his part, had felt an anxiety creeping upon him, fierce and bitter: a need to protect her. When he went out into the city with that grief behind his eyes, saw the sorrows around him, and when he went to the Temple to declare the words God had found for him, haranguing the priests on the white-baked stone steps, he felt keenly around him all the lives he was not doing enough for, but especially hers.

———

On that last morning of their lives together, Yirmiyahu lay beside her, his body bruised and battered, and thought of what must come. Those who had beaten him would seek her out as well. The night before, they had pursued him through the street even to the door of this house. He shuddered. His mind flinched at the thought of Miriam cast to the earth, bloodied and stoned. His heart pounded within him, his hands made fists around the bedding, and she stirred beside him at the movement. Yirmiyahu was breathing harshly. He searched inside his mind, frantic, maddened, like a man rushing about within a house with no windows and a lion barring the door, throwing himself bodily into one wall, then another, searching for some other exit. But there was no other. There was only one.

"What is wrong?" Her voice beside him was soft with sleep.

He relaxed his hands, and calm came over him, cold as winter. There was only one door in this house. He accepted it. He had to, because he was not strong enough to bear seeing her body broken in the dust, beaten and torn by jagged stones. He rolled to his side and then got to his feet, not looking at her. He couldn't, not yet. "Get dressed," he said, his voice cool and distant.

"Yirmiyahu?" Worry in her voice.

He moved about the small, lovely house, slowly but with purpose. He took out the little wooden box in which he kept his coin and spread a woolen cloak beside it, a winter garment he hadn't needed to wear in months. He opened the box and emptied it out, all of it. A music of metal, coins clacking against each other and then thudding into soft, heavy wool. He let his hand rest for a moment on the empty box; his eyes traced its ornate carvings.

It was a rich little thing, a parting gift from his grandmother when he left Anathoth. It had been in the family, she'd said. "Your mother's mother's mother's mother kept her little wooden gods inside it." The skin around her eyes had crinkled with amusement. "If my parents had not betrothed me to a levite," she said, "I might still be keeping little wooden gods inside it. But it has been consecrated for other uses now."

Yirmiyahu trailed his fingers across the little coins. Few enough, yet more than many in the city had. Keeping them in the box—was that another idolatry? Had there been moments when these coins had been to him like small metal gods? Governing his life, choosing his paths for him? Had he prized comfort and this little house with his wife more than his responsibility as *navi*? If the *navi* was to urge the People to become worthy of women like his wife, he must throw himself even in the path of stones. He could *not* do that here, in this house, where some stones might fly past him and strike his wife.

For the briefest moment, his hand stilled over the coins. His heart raced. He thought of bowing before the priests, wearing again the white robes. Residing in safety in this home with Miriam, until their lives were blessed at last with children. This would mean refusing to be *navi*, turning a deaf ear to God's cries in the night for the lovers who'd forsaken her. Yet even if he *could* do that thing, even if it were possible to shut out the voice of God, he could not do that and remain himself, remain true. Uprooted from truth and Covenant, he would be a man he reviled, a man who disgusted him, a man who could ignore the bruises on the thighs of children and the screams at the summit of Tophet. In time, even Miriam would revile him if he broke Covenant with God, if he became that man.

His lips thinned, and he wrapped the wool around the coins and knotted the cloak tightly to keep them from spilling. He did not need them. He would leave that box empty and let God fill it with her invisible but fertile presence, as she did the Ark in the Temple, leaving no space for other things. Compared with what else Yirmiyahu was giving up this day, these little coins were trivial, quaint objects—curiosities that others had attached importance to, as he himself once had—but in the final measure of little worth.

He felt a touch on his shoulder, a soft hand. He drew in a shuddering breath and blinked back hot tears. He didn't turn to look at her, and his voice was gruff. "I am hated here." His rough hand closed over her smaller one, gripped for a moment, one warm squeeze, and then he removed her hand from his shoulder and got to his feet. His body ached with soreness. "I cannot have you killed with stones in my place, and I cannot say what things God will need me to do, what angers I will provoke in the city." He left the cloak full of coins at his feet and moved to the urn of water that stood near their bedding; he felt her eyes on him as he took up a waterskin—the large goatskin bag he used when he had a long walk to make—and dipped it in the urn, filling it. In the dim light, the reflection of his face was just a shadow on the water; the water was cool and wet on his hands. He stood bent over the urn for a long moment, just breathing. Unwilling yet to lift his head and face her.

"My husband?" That quiver in her voice caught at him. "You are frightening me."

He couldn't delay this. "The coins are for you," he said, his voice rough. "You must go. I will sell the house and send the money after you." He straightened and took up the waterskin. "I am going out to hire a few guardsmen to keep you safe on the road to Anathoth."

"Anathoth?" The word was almost a scream. Suddenly he felt her touch at his waist, her arms moving to hold him; he shrugged her off and strode toward the door, halted at her cry.

"But you cannot send me away! I am your wife!"

Swiftly, she came before him and knelt; in her eyes burned a panic too fierce for words. "Please," she wept. "Please, do not put me away, Yirmiyahu. Husband! I have been with you—in everything—suffering with you. Does it mean nothing to you?"

Yirmiyahu groaned and bent swiftly, taking her arms and pulling her to her feet. He had never seen her so helpless before, not even when she'd lost the child. Never seen her kneel or seen her eyes overfill so openly with tears. She did not even turn away her head; she just looked at him.

Something inside him choked off all words, all explanations. None of them were sufficient or could ever be. None of them could speak his heart to her. He held her eyes with his. "I have to keep you safe."

"Not like this," she whispered. Her eyes flickered with understanding and with terrible grief.

"It will be all right. Miriam." His hands trembled where they grasped her arms. He forced the words out: "I free you of your bond to me, though there is no priest here to affirm it or record it. Go where you will. Be safe, my beloved."

She just gazed at him; it was as though she'd been struck across the face and was now holding terribly still. He gripped her arms once, then released her, turned from her. He felt the burn in his eyes and feared he would weep, too. If he did, he would not be able to refrain from embracing her, from begging her forgiveness for this thing he had to do, this thing he *must* do to keep her safe.

Anger roared up inside him, a lion turned loose; he went to the door, threw it open, and strode through. She did not move or cry out his name, but he felt her gaze on him. He walked out into the street and then on into the tangle of the city, uncaring of where his feet might take him, leaving the house behind. His heart burned within him. He could not keep her here. He *could* not.

But how he'd *wounded* her!

As the lily among the thorns, his love, and he'd—

With a snarl, he quickened his pace until he was almost running. There were curses hurled after him as he jostled his way through the people in the street—the sweaty, reeking river of the living who made the rough stones of the street smooth with their hundreds of feet. He needed to find guardsmen he could hire, but first he craved only a moment alone, to breathe, to—

He threw himself into a side alley and against the shaded clay wall of a shop. Slammed his open palms against it. "*God!*" he shrieked. "*God!*"

Sobs grabbed hold of his chest and squeezed his breath and his life into something as small and tense as a wrung towel; he cried and beat at the wall; he fought for breath in small gasps. When he could he screamed again: "*God!*"

A hot wind blew down the street; he didn't heed the glances of passersby who covered their faces with their hoods or street veils, if they were women, and hurried past. For a moment he felt the warm breath of the air on his skin and at his ear, like God's breath. *I am with you always*, the breath whispered. *Even now, even now, Yirmiyahu.*

"I have broken covenant with my wife," Yirmiyahu whispered back, a moan rising in his throat. "I have broken covenant with my wife."

The wind brought no answer to his ears or to his heart.

Yirmiyahu slid to his knees and leaned his head against the wall, pressing the side of his face against the cool clay. His shoulders shook, and he spent the rest of the day there.

———

Yirmiyahu's head jerked up. With terrible lucidity, he saw the mud in the well, the cold walls, felt the thirst in his throat. Panic seized him. He was going to die here.

With a cry, he forced himself to his feet, though the exertion threw him into such dizziness that he thought he'd vomit. His stomach heaving, he faced the wall, searching with his fingers. Stone, mortared and polished smooth by long years of holding water. His fingertips found small cracks, tiny ledges; gasping, he gripped them. Wrenched his foot from the mud with a sound like something spewed from the stomach of a sea creature. His numb toes slid along the stones. Whimpering and muttering, he tried to pull himself up by his fingertips, thinking his toes might find some higher purchase.

Nothing. He lost his grip and slid into the mud, his fingers badly scraped. He moaned and beat the wall with his hands. Bent his head, his forehead against smooth stone. Breathing hard, he muttered a quick, urgent prayer. He'd been taught that God was to be found in all the depths of the earth, in every place. She must be here, too. Though one of his eyes was swollen too dry to make tears, Yirmiyahu wept and begged.

Why had God let him be cast in here? How terribly had he failed as her *navi*? Had she utterly left the city, driven from it by the desecration of her children?

He quieted, listened. He heard only his own panting in the horrible silence of the well.

Roaring hoarsely, he lurched to his feet again, scrambled at the wall, fighting it in a panic, reaching for holds, anything. He got his toes into a crevice no wider than a coin, reached for a higher handhold, pressing his fingertips against the stone, wheezing as he searched. Nothing—nothing! His calf trembled from the strength it took to keep gripping the rock with his toes. He reached farther over his head, then groped far to the left, then to the right along the smooth stone. He found shallow impressions in the rock, nothing he could use to pull himself up. Tilting back his head, he gazed at the circle of daylight far above him. Almost more than anything else, more than water or food, he wanted that light. He wanted to stand in an open place, tilt back his head, and feel the sun's heat on his eyelids. He howled, a bestial cry of need that echoed in the well but brought no answer.

His leg gave out; he collapsed, fell over one of the corpses, shoved himself off it in horror. Losing his balance, he tumbled to the side, plunging his face into the dark, sucking mud. A moment of desperate terror, then he lifted his head and got to a crouch and pressed his back to the stone wall, his knees drawn up. Frantic, he scrubbed mud from his face with the heels of his hands. His eyes stung as he wiped the muck from them. The rot in the well assailed his nostrils anew; he beat at his face with his hands, moaning. He was alone, alone. He would die here. He drew his knees close and shut his eyes, praying again, muttering. "We are the People of the Covenant," he rasped. "Made in the likeness of God." Tapped the back of his head against the wall, as a child does when frustrated, a child who is too young to speak. "We are the People of the Covenant," he groaned, "the spouse of the Giver of Life. None of us lost, none of us forgotten. We are her own."

He fell silent, listened for some trace of that small whisper of God. Then prayed again. He kept tapping his head against the stone.

———

Darkness again.

He blinked his eyes but could not see. He tried to cry out—*adonai, adonai, my God, my God*—but his throat was too parched. He was shivering, though he felt hot as an iron blade set too near a fire. He touched his skin with fingers caked with mud; he burned. He became aware of wetness about his belly and sides; he was sitting slumped in the mud, leaning forward over his knees with his feet planted on what must be sound earth under the mud. Only that position and the cramped immobility of his bent legs was keeping him upright.

For a long, long time he wept. He sat in a world of wet and shadow, of *hoshekh* that clung to the skin and seeped inside him. *Miriam*, he croaked. *Miriam*.

He would never forget his last sight of her. Those eyes overfull with tears. She had always been overfull with love; in loving her and then leaving her, he had taken hold of her and crushed that love from her, until her tears came out at the eyes like that, a terrible wound he had given her, whom he loved.

His lips formed, almost soundlessly, the words his throat could not make. *Adonai, oh adonai. Giver of Life, Sacred Womb, Maker of all that lives and moves. The kings have failed the People. The prophets, too. I failed Miriam. I failed you. I am dying in a dry well. It is over. Who will take responsibility for this People? What* navi *will be there to preserve whatever can be preserved of the city and the land?*

Whether in echo of his own despairing thoughts or in answer to them, remembered words sounded in his heart: *Would that all God's People were prophets.* That was Miriam. Miriam had said that. She'd been quoting Moseh, the great Lawgiver who'd led their ancestors out of the desert with many wonders, and given them the *mitzvot* to keep justice among their tribes and keep the People clean of the dead.

Would that all God's People were prophets. Spoken as she crouched over a pot making a stew. Yirmiyahu had seated himself across from her that night. He was talking of—things. The walking dead that had begun to appear. The famishing of widows and children in the city outside their small house. It was months yet before the start of the siege. "People do not feel safe," he was telling her. He'd been younger then, bewildered but confident that the city would be saved, the People brought back to the Covenant. He'd been sure even the levites would listen, if he just went often enough to the Temple steps.

He had not yet seen the hill of Tophet.

"People do not feel safe in their own city. Miriam, my Miriam, there are children starving, alone. Easy prey for the dead. And I think there are more dead in the city than we think." He chewed on his knuckles a moment—a nervous trait he'd later drop entirely after Tophet, after sending Miriam away, after his heart became smaller and harder inside him. But back then he'd chewed his knuckles often, for though the words God found for him filled him and sustained him, the evil, the hunger, the injustice he was asked to stand and proclaim against bewildered him and filled him with an anxiety and a longing for people to *hear*.

On the other side of the cookpot, Miriam's face was aglow, not only with the sweat of laboring over the stew but also, as Yirmiyahu realized later, with the pregnancy she'd just become aware of, the pregnancy she would tell her husband about later that night—a blessing and a joy that, like Yirmiyahu's faith that the priests could be won over, would be all too brief.

"Miriam," he murmured, barely aware of the brightness in her eyes, so strong were the doubts seeping into him. He had been *navi* only a few short months. God's words still came rarely to him, and still only at night. In truth, Yirmiyahu felt alone, a *navi* whose words caused gasps of dismay but who, in the end, had *only* those few words to sway a weary and neglectful People to any active mending of the Covenant. "This is not like the old days. I am not like one of the old prophets. Eliyahu called fire from heaven to cleanse the land; the undead withered and crumbled to ash. And Devora the Old—though no fire fell from the sky, she razed half the vineyards of Israel before the land was cleansed. She did it, though. And there were—healings."

He shook his head. These tales had been passed down from grandfather to grandson and from grandmother to granddaughter through centuries of levites. Now, for the first time, he wondered whether all of that had really happened, if the *navi* in the past had ever truly stood before the People or against the dead with anything other than words from God. "Healings, Miriam," he murmured, his eyes on the stew, on the bubbling, on something that was certain and could be trusted: when you put hot fluid over coals, it bubbled and a pleasant scent went up. It needed no story from your grandfather for you to trust *that*. Like God's voice in the night, the boiling in the pot was *there*, evident, something a man's own eyes and ears could know.

Yirmiyahu continued reciting the stories, trying to find comfort in the names and acts of each previous *navi*, each prophet who'd mended the Covenant and preserved the People from the ravenous dead. "Yeroboam's hand was bitten, his arm gray—a prophet healed him, calling on the name of God. And a Syrian came to Elisa asking to be healed; he was already shaking with it. And Elisa sent him to the river and washed away the bite as though it were only dirt on his skin. And when Menahem the Mad repented and the prophetess Hadassah instructed him to take every walking corpse he could find in the city and impale them on the walls, every last one, until there were eighty-seven in all, writhing and moaning in the morning sun—" Yirmiyahu's voice grew softer; he was seeing with his eyes the horror of it. "*When that was done,*" he whispered, "*all in the city who'd been bitten but had not succumbed grew hale again.*"

"My husband." Miriam touched his hand with hers.

He barely noticed; his eyes saw other things. "I am no prophet like Elisa or Hadassah," he said. "I have only words and no other gift, no power to heal the bitten or feed the starving. When I pray—" He bit, and a little blood ran from his knuckles. "When I pray, God only sends more words. What good are words when we need a gift like Elisa's?" He pressed his fingers to his temples. "What kind of *navi* am I, Miriam?"

"A dutiful one," she murmured after a moment, "a man who keeps Covenant and asks others to, a man the People need right now, a man I love." Miriam gripped his fingers, squeezed them. "You don't have to contend with eighty-seven dead, as Hadassah did, or with hordes out of the northern cedars, as Devora did. There are only a few dead, and there is grain behind the Temple to feed the city, or most of it," Miriam offered. "If all the priests and all the merchants in this city were men like my husband, all would be well. What the People need is the gift you *do* bring from God, Yirmiyahu—the gift of words that are true, when everyone else plugs their ears with words that are not. Would that all God's people were prophets!"

Her voice was soft, and Yirmiyahu found himself drawn from his doubts to listen; he saw the way her eyes shone, and the sight of it held him, catching at his heart. "If only we all heard the words you hear in our hearts. If only we all listened as passionately, with such suffering, as you do, husband. But most of us can't, and many don't want to." She paused a moment. "I think I feel God in the house sometimes, in the mornings—but I never hear words. Only you do. As a woman," she added softly, "I know how important it is for someone to hear you, and how hard it is. There are so many places where I cannot speak, even if I had a lot to say, and you as my husband must speak for me. I cannot stand in the street like a man and cry out what is in my heart. God can't do this either, I think. She needs you to speak for her. Without your words, the priests would keep her shut away behind that veil in the Temple, the way some husbands shut away their wives, or locked into the Ark; no one would hear her." Her eyes shone above the glow of the fire beneath the cookpot.

"Until all God's people are prophets, your words are all we have, Yirmiyahu."

THIRD DAY: WIND IN THE DARK

HE STARTLED, his body lurching out of a sleep that had been deep but of unknown duration. The hiss was near him in the dark and very loud. His vision was blurred, but he could *hear* it. If it was really there. His hands tightened, and in one of them he felt the slender rib he'd torn from the girl's corpse. A life gift from a man's body to a woman's, that rib could now be converted in the brutality of this well into a weapon. His unclean hand grasping the rib, he again felt feverish with shame, complicit in all the defilements of his city. He hacked from his scorched throat and rolled onto his knees, almost falling into the mud.

That hiss!

The thing had not seized him yet; perhaps it was less mobile even than the last had been. A desire to live roared up inside his chest like a monster bursting into life, fierce and undeniable, though it had not been there a moment before. He blinked desperately, could see a dark form only an arm's length away. He threw himself at it, certain he would feel teeth cutting into his arm but just as certain that if he delayed but a moment he would find himself half-conscious again, helpless food for the broken thing that would eventually crawl or wriggle near enough to feed.

This was the most terrible of his struggles in the well.

It was a scuffling, a wrestling without sight or even clarity of mind; just two human bodies, one dehydrated and shaking, the other too broken to permit the use of more than one limb—just two bodies tumbling and tearing at each other in the mud and the dark. Brutal, silent, except for Yirmiyahu's labored breathing and the other thing's hissing and biting on air. Yirmiyahu stabbed again and again with the sharp rib, piercing perhaps the creature's neck, upper chest, or even face, but whatever demon gave it the semblance of life did not perish. For one instant that jolted through him like a silent scream, Yirmiyahu felt the thing's teeth scrape across his bare shoulder, but he was rolling with it on top of him, and a knee pressed up into its belly sent it tumbling to the side into the mud. A wordless, rasping cry, and the *navi* threw himself back on top of it, driving the rib down like a spear. One dry, cold hand clutched at his arm, pulling his wrist toward snapping teeth; Yirmiyahu caught a reflection of the distant sun in two gray, scratched eyes. That was enough to orient him. With his other hand he grasped the thing's hair, holding its head still. Its strength was terrible, but he forced his arm up above its jaws and twisted and drove the rib hard between its eyes. The thing bucked under him.

Then it was still. No last rattle of breath in the throat. Only stillness. Yirmiyahu collapsed over it like a spent lover, and for a while everything—the corpse, the mud, the well, the city outside, God—everything simply stopped existing.

He did not even dream.

———

He woke as dry as though he'd swallowed the sun and it had caught in his throat. For a long stretch of uncounted and unaccountable time, he gazed up the sheer sides of the well. It was difficult to conceive of any world but the cracked stone walls and the still, cold form beneath him and the distant circle of sunlight and heat, as untouchable as a bird and silent as a mirage in the desert.

Desert. That circle of heat was a portent. They had failed the Covenant; God was leaving her city as it became defiled and uninhabitable, leaving to the desert the People she'd once called from it. The city would become a haunt of owls and jackals who, at least, would prove faithful to their purpose and less quick to devour their own. Yirmiyahu wanted to call out to God, but his body was spent, and in weary dread he felt sure his prayers would only echo unheard in the hollowness of the well.

He lay on the dead; he could feel the hard stillness of it keeping him half-propped out of the mud. It was cold, rigid; the touch of its breast against him was like the touch of a stone in winter. He was shivering, though he only just now realized it. He thought about that for a while, tried to muster the strength of will to lift himself.

Somewhere up there the city was dying. He wondered whether the guards who'd come for him had let Baruch go. And what might have become of the children? Baruch had been teaching them when the guards came in the evening; the children had let out cries of dismay. Baruch had just risen to his feet, silent and impassive, a man carved out of a cliff wall. Seizing Yirmiyahu by the arms, the guards had pulled him out through the door, not even bothering to bind him. The *navi*'s last glance over his shoulder had been at Baruch and the children framed in the doorway: so many eyes on him.

What would become of them all? He had seen dead shuffling along in the alleys they passed as the guards pulled him toward the king's house. How many were there now? And how long would the city's walls stand? Would there be only dead within when the Babylonians finally breached them?

He lifted himself up on his hands, sobbing with the effort. He needed to get away from this body. It reeked; everything reeked of death. There was too much death, too much. He wanted only to hurl himself into the cool mud, and if he died there and the slithering things beneath it ate him, it was enough: he would be content. So long as he did not have to look with his own eyes on any more unclean death.

Breathing hard, he glanced down at the corpse.

His breath caught. Everything in him stilled.

For a long, long time, he just stared at the torn, defiled face.

A terrible sound came from his throat, a sound he had never heard a living being make. A low keen, a moan as heavy with yearning as the wailing of the dead. It was like the scream a hare makes when a farmer has caught it and is beating it with a great stick to kill it. That madness scream before the hare falls into the burrow that has no bottom, the burrow that keeps plummeting all the way down to death. Yirmiyahu lifted mud-caked fingers, cupped the dead face in his palm, the flesh of it so cold it sucked the heat from his hand; it was as though a hole had been punched right through him, and now wind was rushing through the dark in his belly. The moan in his throat rose to a shriek that tore up everything in his chest and left only jagged streamers of flesh and spirit.

It was her face. Hers. Miriam. His wife.

It was her face.

It was shattered, it was distorted, the eyes emptied of everything and flesh torn from her, but it was her; he knew that face, he couldn't be mistaken. It was her.

She'd come back, then. Somehow, before the siege began. She'd come back to the city, or had never actually left—she'd come to find him, perhaps come even to their old house.

But she hadn't found him; somewhere within the city, the dead had found her.

Yirmiyahu screamed until his throat was raw with it. He fell to his side, his hands cupping her head, pressed his face into her shoulder, unable to look at those dead eyes. He kept screaming, and then he could make no sound at all; and still he screamed, his mouth open without any sound but the rasp of escaping breath.

THIRD NIGHT: AS PAPYRUS BURNS

AT THE well's bottom, Yirmiyahu lay without waking, his body racked with cold and dryness. In the city above, the walking corpses fed and felt no remorse for the cries or the panic of the living. This was a night of the dead, in a city of the dead. He knew it, he knew it. *Hoshekh*. Surely God had left the city, fled the People who'd forsaken her, left them to lie in their *hoshekh*, lost and faithless. Surely everything above him was dead. In this well, in this clammy dark, he couldn't know if there were any breathing people yet above him. If he were to cry out now, would the guards hear—and ignore—him, or would only the dead hear the cries of God's *navi*? He couldn't know.

To wake fully would be unbearable. Yet what dream or words out of the past could aid him in this moment? His mind fled through memories that were recent but held no comfort.

———

Zedekiah had held the scroll in his own hands and let it burn. The fire licked and chewed at the edges as he unrolled it slowly over the candle he'd brought to Yirmiyahu's cell. Letting the flame spread a shadow of crackling darkness across the tiny lines of black text.

It took three men to restrain Yirmiyahu. He screamed and kicked, throwing his torso from side to side as though to wrench his arms loose of their bindings by brute strength, like Samson of old, whom no cords could restrain unless he'd first been held and gentled in a woman's arms.

Yirmiyahu threw back his head and howled; still the men held him. Still the little scroll burned; the young king unrolled it a little at a time, watching the slow creep of the flames, inexorable and destructive as pestilence. In desperation, the prophet turned his head and seized on the throat of one of the guards, biting, digging in hard with his teeth, his mouth filling with the taste and scent of human blood; the guard cried out shrilly, and in a moment the others had torn Yirmiyahu loose and cast him to the earthen floor. A sandaled foot slammed down between his shoulder blades, holding him still. He growled and spat; a guard shoved the butt of a spear into the back of his head.

Then he lay still, his eyes open, the room unsteady to his gaze. In a kind of stupor, he watched the king feed Baruch's scroll to the flame, one column of ink at a time. The fire's hunger was too hot now for the candle's thin wick; the flame was too high. The candle melted even as Yirmiyahu watched, wax streaming down its sides. It shortened and shrank even as the flames fed upon the scroll, for fire is the only one of God's creatures that eventually grows thinner and smaller the more it devours.

In the end Zedekiah flicked his fingers, dropping the last crinkling bit of ash onto the earthen floor. Yirmiyahu watched a few flakes of ash drift on the air.

The earth was cool against his cheek.

Sandaled feet stepped into his vision—fine sandals, studded with tiny gems, so that they startled the eyes. He stared dully, hearing the king's voice above him.

"I want you to make me a vow, Yirmiyahu. I want you to vow you will never again make such a scroll. On pain of death—not for you but for the scribe you hire."

Without lifting his head, Yirmiyahu wetted his lips and spat on the sandaled feet. Then the hard weight of a spear slammed into the back of his head again, and he fell off the floor and into a dark place.

———

Baruch had tried to warn him. Scrolls, those children of God's lips and men's hands, were as fragile as the children of women's bodies. They might be devoured as easily, lost as easily, forgotten as easily. If a people could forget the pain in the eyes of children, they could forget God. And if a people could forget God, they could forget the words she gave. If they could forget the words she gave, they could forget the pain in the eyes of children.

———

"We must make a new scroll." His lips were parched and cracked. Savage pain in the back of his head where the spear had struck him. "Miriam, we have to tell Baruch. Miriam, tell Baruch."

The hand that had been dabbing his brow with a cool, damp cloth paused. The voice near his ear was deep and resonant. Baruch's voice. "Miriam isn't here, friend. You sent her away."

Yirmiyahu coughed once. "Why would I do that?"

The cloth dabbed again, now at his eyelids. It felt very cool, very soothing, though only when it touched his closed eyes did he realize how hot, how seared they had been. "Hush, friend. Rest now; you were beaten badly. We can talk later."

———

In his sleep, Yirmiyahu heard a woman humming, somewhere near. It was a soft sound, very beautiful. It made him think of his grandmother, in his father's house at Anathoth, and how as a child he'd wakened often to the sound of her humming as she worked at her loom by the window, bright threads of dyed wool moving through her fingers. She was always humming lullabies, even when it was morning and the world was waking; perhaps she felt the world was too much awake and ought to doze more of the time. He remembered sometimes sitting in her lap as a small child while she hummed, while his father, her son, was away, sacrificing a white bull or an unblemished goat in atonement for the uncleanness of the people or in honor of the blessings given him by the Giver of Life. Yirmiyahu remembered his grandmother's scent of dried rosemary, and the way her humming sometimes bloomed like a sunflower and became her voice, a soft voice unroughened by age.

> Sleep, my child, sleep,
> And I will sing to thee
> Of the sun and the rain
> And the sycamore tree
> And the ships that walk on the sea.

Yirmiyahu opened his eyes, found himself staring up at stout rafters of cedar, warm with sunlight. A white butterfly, no larger than his thumbnail, was hovering about one of the rafters, its wings opening and closing like a child's hands. Yirmiyahu felt a wool blanket gentle and warm under his fingertips. He drew in breath slowly, then breathed out. Sore, he sat up; he was in a little wooden room with a high window. This wasn't the house of Baruch the scribe. And it wasn't the house he'd shared with Miriam his wife in Yerusalem before the siege, or the house he'd shared with her for a short time in Anathoth. This was *his* room, his own room in the home of his childhood, in that sturdy old house of cedar, his father's house, a place of safety and surety. At the table in the next room, he'd learned to read, tracing his fingertip gently over the lines of hard, angular letters in his father's scroll of the Law, the only scroll the town possessed. Though his writing had always been slow and halting, he could read more swiftly even than his father, or any of the other levites in his father's town. He used to stand at the doorstep of this house after dark, looking out over the fields by moonlight and reciting the *mitzvot*, the many rules of the Law, in a rumbling Hebrew dialect that was now centuries old but very beautiful.

He flung the blanket aside; he was in his loincloth. Sliding his legs from the low bed, he felt the cool wood floor against his feet. He sucked in his breath; the firmness of that wood was strange to him. How long had it been since he'd slept above a wooden floor rather than an earthen one?

He could still hear a woman humming faintly; his grandmother must be at her loom. He pressed his hands to the thin mattress and pushed himself to his feet. The rafters were just above his head; his hair brushed them—this room was smaller than he recalled. He swayed a moment, caught at one of the beams with his hand. He stood there sweating—why was his body so weary?—and listened, listened. The humming became song, and his eyes widened. He realized that the sound wasn't coming from within the house. It was coming through the window, from outside. And it was a voice he knew.

His heart raced. "Not grandmother," he whispered. "Miriam."

Without losing another moment, he hurried from the room and darted through the dining chamber, his hip colliding with the table in his haste. He reached the door, hurled it open, threw himself out into sunlight so bright it seared his eyes and left him standing, blinking, in the grass.

He heard her laughter, high-pitched and sweet, and in a moment felt her warm, small hand take his, and another hand pressed over his eyelids; afterimages still danced hot and white against the dark of his lids. He moaned with the pain of it.

"You'll be all right, husband." Her voice, near his ear. "But how funny you looked, leaping from the house in your loincloth, like you were on fire!"

"I *am* on fire," he murmured.

She laughed again, and he felt the softness of her lips pressed to his. It overwhelmed him, so that tears stung against his eyelids—or perhaps that was the pain from the sun. The sun felt hot against his brow, and he knew they would need to find shade in a moment. But for this moment he simply relished the touch of her smooth hand against his eyelids and the taste of her mouth.

When she took her hand from his eyes and he opened them, blinking, they were seated together on a cool white stone in the shade of a tall terebinth with branches that seemed to spread a roof of leaves across half the sky. He remembered that tree; his father used to read passages from the Law to him beneath it.

He looked at his wife. She was young; she looked as she had when they first met. Her hair was dark in the shade, her eyes darker; he couldn't stop gazing at them. His lips were parted; he was rapt. Her small hand he held in his. Somewhere across the fields that stretched wide and free about his father's house and the nearby village of Anathoth, he could hear a herdsman singing, a sound faint and lovely.

The leaves of the terebinth above them moved without any breeze, and he was speared by the cold certainty that he was asleep and dreaming—and that this wasn't any night dream but a true dream. There was a vividness to it, a reality to the ache in his hip where he'd hit the table, the warmth of Miriam's hand in his. His heart beat within him. He felt, with that utter and complete certainty that only comes in dreams, that Miriam was truly visiting him—to say good-bye—and that when he woke he would not see her again.

"Miriam," he whispered.

She smiled, her eyes moist; then her face crumpled. "I missed you."

Almost shyly, he reached out, touched her hair, then caressed it. "Forgive me," he whispered.

"You wanted me to go." Her eyes were deep. "I—I couldn't. I got as far as the gate, then dismissed the man you sent with me. I went back into the city. I went to find you." Her face flushed, and Yirmiyahu could feel her anger like lightning in the air. "You had no right to send me away. I am not a dog, Yirmiyahu, or a donkey, or a packet of dried herbs you can return to my mother because you're afraid you'll only lose it."

"I know." He took one of her hands in his, gripped it, his face contorted with the violence of the feelings within him, with the strain of trying to pour into words something that mere physical, animal sounds could never contain or convey. "I was afraid for you—"

"In all that city, what could you need more than me at your side?" Her eyes flashed. "And what could I need more than your arms around me and your heart listening to me? Yirmiyahu! We were going to have *children* together—if we could."

"I know," he whispered again.

The terebinth faded from sight; everything became a feature-less gray. There was only her, and in a moment she would be gone, too. Yirmiyahu cried out and pulled her to him, held her tight, felt her tense. Then her body relaxed and she shook with silent sobs. He breathed raggedly himself, unable to bear the sweetness and the pain of this moment. Everything tight, painfully tight, in his chest. He crushed her to him, breathed in the scent of her hair, felt her warmth in his arms, whispered her name again and again.

"I love you," he said hoarsely.

"And I you," she wept. "I you, my husband."

—

Sunlight came through the cracks in the boards over the window, sharp splinters of light that made his eyes sting. He lifted his hand but could still see the light through his fingers. He drew in breath slowly, the loss of her a violence in his chest. His head turned from the window; Baruch was sitting there beside the blanket on which he lay. When their eyes met, Baruch nodded once, though his face showed no other expression.

Yirmiyahu moved his lips to speak, but his throat was too dry.

"We are under house arrest, friend," Baruch said quietly. "The king is merciful." His lip twisted.

Yirmiyahu shut his eyes a moment. Already the dream was slipping from his mind, like bright foliage torn away and riding the wind into the distance. The ache in his chest. He swallowed once. He had to put away thoughts of her. The memory of the past days—the burning of the scroll—it all came back. There was work to do. There was always work to do. More now than before.

He was *navi*.

Yirmiyahu tried to get up; the room spun. Baruch's gentle hand on his breast pushed him back. "Lie still," his friend murmured.

"Have to"—a hoarse croak—"another scroll—and copies—many as we can—"

"You do that, my friend, and they will bury you somewhere. That young king will drop you into some dry well and leave you there until this city is nothing but ash." Baruch's voice was firm, as uncompromising as the hand that kept Yirmiyahu down. Yirmiyahu clutched at his friend's wrist, though his fingers seemed weak as twigs. He had to get up. He had to speak the words God had spoken to him—for this he had given up Miriam, sending her away while he remained here. He had to keep going. Had to—

"Help me," he rasped.

Baruch didn't move his hand. His voice was intense, more impassioned than Yirmiyahu had ever heard him speak. "It is only a miracle of your God that you are alive—God, and my begging at the king's door. It is over, Yirmiyahu."

Yirmiyahu's lip curved grimly; he felt consciousness slipping from him and fought it. "Only when I'm dead," he growled as he fell.

———

He woke with a start, shaking. It was dark, utterly dark. He threw out his hands, felt cold stone around him, hard and immovable. The well. He was in the well. The burning of the scroll, waking in Baruch's house, that conversation with the scribe—all of it many weeks past. His heart pounded. In the midst of those memory dreams, he'd been sent a *true* dream beneath the waving branches of the terebinth: he was certain of it. Miriam had visited him in his sleep. Coughing clawed into his throat and he bent over, hacking into the mud, his insides trying to hurl themselves up his throat and out into the well.

When he could breathe again, wheezing in the dark, he felt around slowly; his hand found the cold chest of one of the corpses, which lay almost against his side in the mud. He needed no light to tell him which one this was; his heart told him. Shaking still, breathing in great rasps, he lay over the body. His hands moved up the still form, remembering her, until they found her face, which was slick with mud; he gripped her head but could not turn it. His fingers found her still, hard eyes and traced the large roundness of her nose, which he had always loved and which by some marvel had survived her death intact. He ran his hands up over her brow and found her head shattered, punctured, and tears burned his eyes. He found her lips with his thumb and traced them; they were no longer soft as they had been in life. Weeping, he kissed her. Taking her lower lip between his lips, he kissed her gently, tasting mud and old blood. The reek of her was sickeningly sweet in his nostrils; he ignored it and kissed her as lovingly, as yearningly, as he had on their first night. Until his next coughing fit seized him and shook him like a rabbit in a jackal's jaws.

He hadn't been there when she perished. That was the only thought that could grip the slick, sliding surface of his mind. With the same clarity and certainty with which he'd seen her in the true dream, beneath the terebinth—a *navi*'s clarity in seeing what had been or what would be—he now saw her walking in the city, her eyes swollen from tears. Saw how Miriam had returned to find him, unwilling to leave him, the man she had suffered with and loved, the man she was covenanted to. She'd found their house dark and empty, its new owner not yet moved in; from the door she'd called out her husband's name. There'd been a noise, a clatter in the other room, a thump against the wall. "Yirmiyahu?" she'd called. She'd stepped carefully through the dark, looking for him. She'd nudged open the door to their bedchamber, where they'd made love so many nights, and other nights simply fallen asleep holding each other, and still other nights gone to sleep with their backs to each other, their hearts pierced by anger or guilt from some fight left unfinished. Her small fingers had touched the wood of the door, nudged it open. With a creak it had swung inward. She peered through it, in the dim light from the room's small window, light torn by the broken, snapped, violated slats of wood that had half barred it; something had torn or smashed through them. Beneath the window, in its faint, shredded light, she could glimpse a shape crouching.

"Yirmiyahu?" Her voice softer, with fear.

The shape had straightened slowly, its eyes glinting in the dim light. Its hands lifting. A low groan in the dark as it took an unsteady step toward her.

Yirmiyahu couldn't see the rest. Perhaps Miriam had frozen in terror, seeing that hulking figure move toward her; perhaps she'd bolted, darting into the other room only to crack her hip against the table and tumble with a shriek to the floor. The vision passed from him, slipping away as swiftly as had the true dream beneath the terebinth.

Yirmiyahu groaned through clenched teeth and twined his fingers into her hair. He kissed her again as he wept, leaving tears and mucus on her nose and cheek.

He hadn't been there.

And with a jagged rib, he'd completed the desecration of her body, the defiling of a body holy and beautiful, her body, his wife's body. How completely he had failed her and betrayed her.

She'd needed him, she had come for him, she'd come back to find him. And when the unclean dead grasped at her and tore into her, he hadn't been there.

That knowledge roared through him, and in its passing the last certainties inside him lit and cracked and curled like burning papyrus; everything in him simply burned away. He kissed her until the remnants in his chest crumbled into ash; then he lay still, clasping her, half lying in the mud that remained as mute testimony that the empty husk of the well had once been a body filled with water and life.

———

A slow crawl of time that could not be tasted or touched. The three corpses grew colder, the reek of them thicker. Harsh coughing in the well in between those stretches of fitful sleep in which the only sound was the rasp of labored breathing. Then more coughing.

———

Perhaps in the city above—if it were not already lost to the lurching dead—perhaps the new scrolls, the copies Baruch had made, though reluctantly, had found a few voices to recite them on the Temple steps; perhaps some of the younger levites gathered in quiet rooms even now, drawing the slats over the windows, then speaking in hushed whispers of Yirmiyahu's words. It was possible. But in the well Yirmiyahu was bereaved of words. He didn't hear God's quiet voice, comforting him or calling him to his responsibilities as her *navi*. His grief had torn so much out of his chest that he simply lay, unlistening, like a corpse waiting to be stirred.

It was possible that in an hour, or a day, or a week, if he still breathed, the guards might pull him out, shivering like a child from the womb. Perhaps God would speak then; perhaps she would gift him with new words, words that would cup him as a woman's warm hands might cup an infant, holding him, words of such promise and hope that they could replenish both his heart and this drying and dying city. Or perhaps, though no words should come, were he to be pulled into the brightness of the day above and into the fierce light of God's presence, he might yet emerge from the well with a primal scream, a raw shriek capable of conveying the horror and loss of every severing of bond and covenant that men or women had suffered since the first birth. This was possible. The silence in the well might be the silence of utter bereavement or the silence before birth. In the fertility of her heart, God's capacity for giving birth and loving rebirth might still be greater than any death—if she hadn't left the city entirely. Or if she had but might yet come back, even as Miriam had come back from the gate, and if she survived her return, as Miriam hadn't. Yirmiyahu didn't know. He could no longer hear God weeping behind her veil. He could no longer hear anything but his own labored breathing.

———

Yirmiyahu lay over his dead wife, hollow and still. The well filled with death as with dark water and with darkness that filled the mouth and nostrils until he lay completely still, the fire in his ribs snuffed out. His body almost forgot to breathe. In this hole in the city there was neither pain nor sorrow nor regret nor memory of joy. The world was cold and filled with the hungry and the dead, and in the numb *hoshekh* of time everything was lost and nothing recovered. In the lethal, irremediable quiet, Yirmiyahu waited without thought or movement for the whisper of God's voice or the rattle of a dying breath in his throat. Waiting in the silence, waiting in the silence.

ACKNOWLEDGMENTS

A PROJECT *like* The Zombie Bible *is a fearful undertaking and requires the aid, goodwill, encouragement, and advice of many people. I offer my deepest gratitude…*

To Andrew Hallam, for his diligent and enthusiastic reading of my work; to Jeff VanderMeer, my editor, for his insight; to all those who generously gave feedback on excerpts; to my pastor, for his encouragement and prayer; to Alex Carr and the remarkable team at 47North; and to Danielle Tunstall, for graciously permitting me the use of her art.

To the cast and crew of the good ship Qdoba, *who during one critical summer, were quick to offer me a quiet corner in which to write during many lunch breaks.*

To the many writers who have moved my heart or inspired my mind, not least among them C. J. Cherryh, for Merchanter's Luck; *Gene Wolfe, for* Soldier of the Mist; *Max Brooks, for* World War Z;

Kim Paffenroth, for Valley of the Dead; *Orson Scott Card, for* Seventh Son; *and to the many writers, known and unknown, who have labored across so many centuries to deliver to us here, this day, that magnificent and often bewildering record and love letter we call the Bible.*

To my wife, Jessica, and my daughters, River and Inara—it can't always be easy living with a husband and father whose mind wanders with such frequency into daydreams of the hungry dead, or who leaps often from his chair to scribble a note; if it were not for their patience, their laughter, and their love, you would not now be holding this work in your hands.

And to all of you, my readers—it is you who make these stories breathe.

A NOTE ON NAMES

IN REVIVING these ancient stories, I have chosen in most cases to use the Hebrew (usually Tiberian) for the names of places and people. Hence *Yirmiyahu* and *Moseh*. However, I've allowed some inconsistency.

For some names I have retained a variant because it sounded better to my ears: hence *Samson* instead of *Simson* and *Devora* instead of *Deborah*. I have sometimes retained an anglicized version of a lesser-known name (like *Zedekiah*) because an entire character had long ago grown up in my mind around the English name.

In one case (*Yerusalem*), I have chosen a hybrid between the English and the Hebrew. The change of consonant allows the city to feel less familiar to the modern reader (which is essential if the reader is to set aside enough modern preconceptions about

Jerusalem to enjoy the story) while still retaining some of the cultural significance and power of the name "Jerusalem," which would be lost for most non-Hebrew speakers if I used the more beautiful and linguistically accurate name *Yerushalayim*.

In these few cases, I have permitted my instincts as a story-teller to take precedence over my fastidiousness as a scholar.

ABOUT THE AUTHOR

Stant Litore doesn't consider his writing a vocation; he considers it an act of survival. As a youth he witnessed the 1992 outbreak in the rural Pacific Northwest firsthand, as he glanced up from the feeding bins one dawn to see four dead staggering toward him across the pasture, dark shapes in the morning fog. With little time to think or react, he took a machete from the barn wall and hurried to defend his father's livestock; the experience left him shaken. After that, community was never an easy thing for him. The country people he grew up with looked askance at his later choice of college degree and his eventual graduate research on the history of humanity's encounters with the dead, and the citizens of his college community were sometimes uneasy at the machete and rosary he carried with him at all times and at his grim look. He did not laugh much, though on those occasions when he did the laughter came from him in wild guffaws that seemed likely to break him apart. As he became book-learned, to his own surprise he found an intense love of ancient languages, a fierce admiration for his ancestors, and a deepening religious bent. On weekends he went rock climbing in the cliffs without rope or harness, his fingers clinging to the mountain, in a furious need to accustom himself to the nearness of death and to teach his body to meet it. A rainstorm took him once on the cliffs and he slid thirty-five feet and hit a ledge without breaking a single bone and concluded that he was either blessed or reserved for a fate far worse. Finding women beautiful and worth the trouble, he married a girl his parents considered a heathen woman but whose eyes made him smile. She persuaded him to come down from the cliffs, and he persuaded her to wear a small covenant ring on her hand, spending what coin he had to make it one that would shine in starlight and whisper to her heart how much he prized her. Desiring to live in a place with fewer trees (though he misses the forested slopes of his youth), a place where you can scan the horizon for miles and see what is coming for you while it is still well away, he settled in Colorado with his wife and two daughters, and they live there now. The mountains nearby call to him with promises of refuge. Driven again and again to history with an intensity that burns his mind, he corresponds in his thick script for several hours each evening with scholars and archaeologists and even a few national leaders or thugs wearing national leaders' clothes who hoard bits of forgotten past in far countries. He tells stories of his spiritual ancestors to any who will come by to listen, and he labors to set those stories to paper. Sometimes he lies awake beside his sleeping wife and listens in the night for any moan in the hills, but there is only her breathing soft and full and a mystery of beauty beside him. He keeps his machete sharp but hopes not to use it.

zombiebible@gmail.com
@thezombiebible
http://zombiebible.blogspot.com